DATE DUE

12/15			
11/15			

16,545

303.48
Pas

Pascoe, Elaine
Mexico and the United States . . .

Dupo High School Library

MEXICO
AND THE
UNITED STATES

MEXICO
AND THE
UNITED STATES

• • •

COOPERATION
AND CONFLICT

• • •

ELAINE PASCOE

TWENTY-FIRST CENTURY BOOKS
A DIVISION OF HENRY HOLT AND COMPANY
NEW YORK

Twenty-First Century Books
A Division of Henry Holt and Company, Inc.
115 West 18th Street
New York, NY 10011

Henry Holt® and colophon are trademarks of
Henry Holt and Company, Inc.
Publishers since 1866

Text copyright © 1996 by Elaine Pascoe
All rights reserved.
Published in Canada by Fitzhenry & Whiteside Ltd.
195 Allstate Parkway, Markham, Ontario L3R 4T8

Library of Congress Cataloging-in-Publication Data
Pascoe, Elaine.
Mexico and the United States: cooperation and conflict / Elaine Pascoe.
p. cm.
Includes index.
Summary: Discusses the relationship between the United States
and Mexico, including economic, cultural, and historical aspects.
1. United States—Relations—Mexico—Juvenile literature.
2. Mexico—Relations—United States—Juvenile literature.
[1. United States—Relations—Mexico. 2. Mexico—
Relations—United States.] I. Title.
E183.8.M6P2 1996
303.48'272073—dc20   96-11430
                                                    CIP
                                                    AC

ISBN 0-8050-4180-X
First Edition—1996

DESIGNED BY KELLY SOONG

Printed in Mexico
All first editions are printed on acid-free paper. ∞
1 3 5 7 9 10 8 6 4 2

Photo credits
p. 20: Bill Ross/Woodfin Camp & Associates; p. 38 (upper left): Corbis-Bettmann; p. 38 (right): Archive Photos; pp. 38 (lower left), 72: AP/Wide World Photos; p. 56: A. Ramey/Woodfin Camp & Associates; p. 88: Najlah Feanny/Saba; p. 98: D. Donne Bryant.

For the Third Thursday group

ACKNOWLEDGMENTS

The author wishes to acknowledge a debt to the reporters, in particular Tim Golden and Anthony DePalma of the *New York Times*, whose firsthand accounts of contemporary events in Mexico and the border region are cited throughout this book. Special thanks also to the reference librarians at the Southbury and New Milford, Connecticut, public libraries for their invaluable assistance.

CONTENTS

1	AT THE BORDER	13
2	SETTLERS AND SOLDIERS	21
3	REVOLUTION, INTERVENTION	39
4	THE MIGRANTS	57
5	DOLLARS AND PESOS	73
6	NEW TIMES, NEW ISSUES	89
7	MEXICO AND DEMOCRACY	99

Mexico and the United States: A Chronology	109
Source Notes	115
Further Reading	119
Index	123

MEXICO
AND THE
UNITED STATES

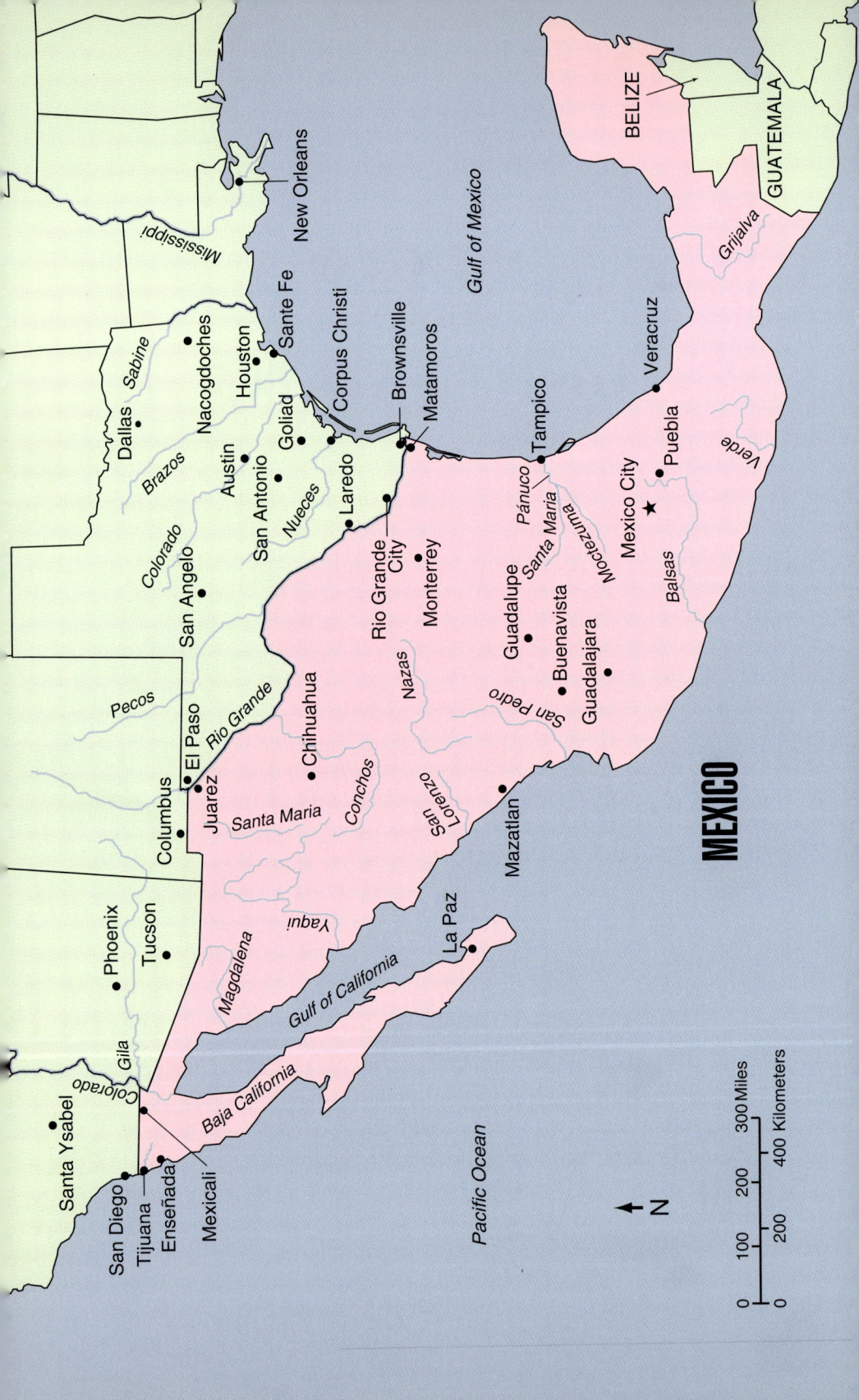

1

AT THE BORDER

Along the flood channel of the Tijuana River, stadium lights turn night into day. More than one hundred people have gathered near the river this night, dressed in dark clothing and sharing a common hope. They are Mexicans who, unable to get permission to enter the United States legally, want to cross the border anyway. First, though, they'll have to find a way over, around, or through the tall metal fence that stares at them forbiddingly from the north.

In the past, crossing the border wasn't difficult for would-be migrants like these—*pollos*, or chickens, in border jargon. It seldom took more than a day or two to find an unwatched place to hop the fence into El Norte. Those who didn't know the way could hire a smuggler—a *pollero*, or coyote—to take them for $100 or so. And once across, it was easy for illegal immigrants to blend into the Hispanic-

American culture of the U.S. Southwest or, with the help of friends and relatives already in the United States, travel anywhere in the country. The lure was employment. Although most illegal immigrants could hope for manual labor and service jobs at best, those jobs were easier to find and paid higher wages than jobs in Mexico.

The lure of employment remains, but for the group waiting at Tijuana, much about the crossing has changed. In the mid-1990s, powerful lights, new fencing, and stepped-up patrols on both sides of the border created daunting obstacles at the most heavily traveled crossing points, such as those between Tijuana and San Diego, California; and Ciudad Juárez and El Paso, Texas. As a result, many in this group have been at the border for weeks waiting for an opportunity to cross, and now they are running out of money. Some have been cheated by *polleros* who took their savings, promising to help them cross, and then disappeared. Still, they might have faced worse. Crime is rampant in the *tierra de nadie* (no man's land) of the Tijuana border, and assault, robbery, and rape are risks the migrants face.

With security so tight, and money running low, several of the migrants are ready to leave Tijuana. They're not ready to give up hope of entering the United States, though. They have decided to try farther east, perhaps crossing into Arizona. The border is less closely watched in rural and desert regions. But the risks are high—there are stories of families who have lost children, and of people who have simply disappeared, attempting a dangerous desert crossing.

• • •

The tractor-trailers are lined up, diesel engines humming at a throaty idle, as they wait to cross the Rio Grande at the International Bridge in Laredo, Texas. The traffic jam is a routine event at this border point. The eighteen-wheelers are packed with machine tools, car parts, computers, factory equipment, and other materials for the growing number of factories and businesses clustered on the Mexican side of the border. And traffic is just as heavy in the other direction. Trucks hauling Mexican-made machinery, electronic products, foodstuffs, and other goods pour across the border and head up I-35 into Texas. Mixed in with the truck traffic are cars filled with shoppers headed for Laredo's Mall del Norte.

This busy border traffic has helped make Laredo a boomtown, one of the fastest growing cities in the United States. The boom was already well under way in 1994, when a new trade agreement took effect. Under the North American Free Trade Agreement (NAFTA), Canada, Mexico, and the United States agreed to gradually eliminate barriers to trade and investment and to allow goods to flow freely across their common borders. Even before the agreement, Mexico was the third-largest trading partner of the United States, drawing two-thirds of its imports from the United States and sending about two-thirds of its exports back over the border. In NAFTA's first year, trade between the United States and Mexico jumped by almost $16 billion.[1]

Businesses on both sides of the border have benefited, and the trade has helped create thousands of jobs. But it has brought problems, too. The Rio Grande and other rivers in the border region are tainted with pollution, and on many days a foul, brownish haze hangs over border cities. Much of the pollution stems from factories, or *maquiladoras*, on the Mexican side. Since the 1970s, U.S. automakers and other manufacturers have set up hundreds of plants there, taking advantage of low Mexican wages and loose environmental restrictions. They are able to ship their products back to the states virtually duty-free. The *maquiladoras* provide jobs for about half a million people—but by moving south of the border, manufacturers have put some American factory workers out of work. And despite the gain in jobs, one-fourth of the people in Mexican border towns live in poverty.[2]

• • •

On a barren strip of land outside Rio Grande City, Texas, a collection of rusty trailers and ramshackle buildings clusters at the end of a dusty dirt road. Nailed together out of scrap lumber, shipping pallets, and tar paper, many of these shacks have no more than one room. There are no sewers and no public water supply; trash litters a slope behind the little settlement because there's no provision for garbage collection. Only a few of the shacks have electricity. This is a *colonia*, or "new settlement"—one of about 1,400 that are scattered along the Rio Grande on the Texas side of the border. The people who live in these settlements are immigrants from Mexico, mostly legal, who hope to achieve what has always been a great American dream: to own a home and a bit of land.[3]

The *colonias* don't fit the picture most Americans have of their country. They're a far cry from the well-groomed suburban developments that ring cities elsewhere in Texas and throughout the United States. Normally, developers are required to pave roads and provide sanitation and utilities. But loopholes in state and local laws (and sometimes lack of enforcement) have allowed the developers of *colonias*, who are mostly wealthy private landowners, to ignore these requirements. And residents seldom take their complaints to the authorities—they know that if they do, they might lose their homes. Most are trying to buy the tiny parcels of land on which their houses stand by paying the developer a bit each month. They're deeply in debt, and the terms of the agreement give the developer the right to evict them at a moment's notice. But the cost of saying nothing is also high: Diseases such as dysentery, tuberculosis, and hepatitis flourish in the unsanitary conditions of the *colonias*.

◆ ◆ ◆

These brief impressions from the 2,000-mile-long border that divides Mexico and the United States only hint at the range and complexity of the relationship between the two countries. Economic, cultural, and historical ties bind Mexico and the United States, and shared interests and mutual problems draw them together. But people on opposite sides of the border often have quite different views of this relationship. Their perceptions are colored by cultural differences, economic disparities, and a history that includes more friction and misunderstanding than cooperation and tolerance.

It isn't easy to be the southern neighbor of the United States, the world's most economically and politically powerful nation. Mexicans look north and see a nation of more than 250 million people, producing $6.5 trillion worth of goods and services a year, maintaining a huge standing army and an arsenal of nuclear weapons. The United States prides itself on being a nation of immigrants, and it comprises an enormous range of ethnic, religious, and political groups. Yet a streak of intolerance and xenophobia—fear of foreigners—has been part of the U.S. makeup from the beginning, and it still sometimes plays a part in the country's dealings with other nations and other peoples. The United States has also often viewed itself as the world's flag bearer in great causes, particularly in the cause of championing democracy. Over the years, this view has led the country to do much good around the world. But at times it has colored U.S. actions with an attitude that other countries see as astounding arrogance.

Americans, for their part, look south and see a nation with a rapidly growing population of about 94 million, where spurts of economic growth have been halted repeatedly by economic crises—and where political unrest is held in check by the government. Many Americans view Mexico as the source of hundreds of thousands of impoverished immigrants, legal and illegal, and look no deeper. There is, however, infinitely more to see.

Mexico is the most populous Spanish-speaking country in the world, with a rich history and a culture that combines Indian and Spanish traditions. Its past reaches back to the kingdoms of the Aztecs and the Mayas, two of the most advanced civilizations of ancient America. For three hundred years, its capital, Mexico City, was the center of the Spanish colonial empire in the Western Hemisphere.

Today Mexico is the third-largest country in Latin America, and Mexico City is the second most populous city in the world. Mexico's land ranges from steamy jungles to snow-capped volcanic peaks, and beneath it lies tremendous wealth—in particular, some of the world's largest oil reserves. That wealth isn't evenly distributed; Mexico has many millionaires, but poverty is widespread, and in the mid-1990s as many as 30 percent of the country's workers were unemployed. Despite deep and abiding social problems, however, Mexico's many assets have helped make it an emerging economic force and a leader in Latin American affairs.

Officially, the United States has long held that Mexican economic strength and political stability are essential to its own national interests, for security along the border as well as for the growth of trade and commerce. Over the years the

United States has taken a variety of steps to help achieve those goals. But in the Mexican view, many of those actions have infringed on Mexican sovereignty and benefited the United States far more than Mexico. In the chapters that follow, we'll see how past conflicts as well as shared experiences have helped shape this relationship, and we'll examine some of the most important issues between the two countries.

Cooperation between Mexico and the United States has become even more important today, because the two countries have forged closer trading ties than at any time in their history. When Mexico is hit by an economic or political crisis, U.S. trade suffers, and U.S. investments plummet in value. Pollution and other environmental problems don't respect international borders; they strike both countries equally. Immigration, law enforcement—in these and in many other areas, growing interdependence makes it more important than ever that Mexico and the United States work together.

The Maya Indians thrived in Mexico between A.D. 250 and 900. This building is a fine example of their architecture.

2

SETTLERS AND SOLDIERS

The history of colonial America, as most people in the United States learn it, begins with the founding of Jamestown, Virginia, by English settlers in 1607. But in 1598—nine years before Jamestown and long before the Pilgrims had even thought of crossing the Atlantic Ocean to settle at Plymouth—a group of Europeans founded a settlement in what would one day be the southwestern United States. The settlers, who were Spanish, had traveled north from Mexico, led by Juan de Oñate. Their settlement, San Juan de los Caballeros, was on the banks of the Rio Grande, near the mouth of the Chama River.

A dozen years later the Spanish founded the city of Santa Fe, not far to the south, to serve as the capital of the province of New Mexico. For more than two hundred years,

Spain would rule not only the region around Santa Fe but a vast portion of the American West, including all or part of the present-day states of California, Nevada, Utah, Arizona, Colorado, New Mexico, and Texas. Then, in 1821, the region would win independence from Spain—as part of Mexico.

In all this time, there was little contact with British North America or, after American independence, the new United States. But by the 1830s, Mexico and the United States were on a collision course. The United States was expanding westward, and Mexican territory was in the way.

THE SPANISH REALM

Before the Spanish, central and southern Mexico were home to highly developed Indian civilizations, the Mayas, Aztecs, and others. The Spanish conquered these peoples and subjugated them. But to the north, the situation was different. With its hot deserts and inhospitable mountains, this area had only a few Indian groups. There was conflict between the Spanish and Indians, to be sure. Santa Fe, for example, was built on the ruins of an Indian pueblo, and Pueblo Indians drove the Spanish out and reoccupied the city from 1680 to 1692. But for the most part the Spanish colonized, rather than conquered, the regions that today are northern Mexico and the U.S. Southwest.

Spanish priests were among the first Europeans to arrive. Along the coast of California, and in inland areas as well, they founded missions that thrived on the labor of Indians. Ranchers and miners followed. But this pattern of colonization, with missions and forts leading the way, didn't work well in areas where Indians or the climate were too hostile. In Texas, for example, the Spanish established just three permanent settlements before 1800—at Goliad, Nacogdoches, and San Antonio.

The new century found the Spanish empire weakened by divisions and conflicts in Europe, and Mexicans fired by the examples of the American, French, and Haitian revolutions. Talk of freedom turned to action on September 16, 1810, when Miguel Hidalgo y Costilla, a priest at the little church of Dolores, called on his parishioners to shake off Spanish rule. The *Grito de Dolores* (call of Dolores), as his speech is known, started the Mexican war for independence.

Hidalgo was captured and executed within a year, but the fighting continued. Finally, ten years after Hidalgo's call to arms, a Spanish officer changed the course of the war. Colonel Augustín de Iturbide defected to the rebel side with 2,500 troops. Other army units followed, and Spain was forced to grant Mexico its independence in 1821.

The first years of independence were tumultuous. Iturbide had himself named emperor, but was thrown out within nine months by General Antonio López de Santa Anna. Under a new constitution, Mexico became a republic and was officially recognized by the United States and most European countries. But the transition was far from smooth. The presidency would change hands some thirty times in as many years, and Santa Anna would take the reins eleven separate times.

Many of the most important events of the revolution and the years immediately after took place in southern and central Mexico, in and around Mexico City. To many people in the north, they were distant rumblings. To be sure, independence brought important changes everywhere in the country. Even in California, the missions declined after new laws stripped the Roman Catholic Church of much of its power.

Independence also ended Spanish restrictions that had severely limited Mexican trade with the United States and other countries. But reaching Mexico's northern territories required weeks of jolting travel over empty, rough terrain or, in the case of California, a dangerous ocean voyage. So these regions remained thinly populated. And, far from the central government in Mexico City, the people developed an independent outlook. Mexico City, meanwhile, was absorbed in its own troubles and paid little attention to events in the north.

Richard Henry Dana was a Boston college student when he sailed aboard a trading ship for Mexican California in 1834. In *Two Years Before the Mast*, he described his voyage around Cape Horn, at the tip of South America, and the society he found on the West Coast. Californians still followed a way of life very close to that of colonial Mexico, with wealthy landowners enjoying great privilege and Indians serving as slaves in all but name.

Dana described the town of Monterey, at that time the home of the governor-general and thus the seat of government for California:

> In the center of [the town] is an open square, surrounded by four lines of one-story plastered buildings, with half a dozen cannon in the centre; some mounted, and others not. This is the "Presidio," or fort. Every town has a presidio in its centre; or rather, every presidio has a town built around it; for the forts were first built by the Mexican government, and then the people built near them for protection. . . . [E]ach town has a commandant, who is the chief military officer, and has charge of the fort, and of all transactions with foreigners and foreign vessels. . . . No Protestant has any civil rights, nor can he hold any property, or, indeed, remain more than a few weeks on shore, unless he belong to some vessel. Consequently, the Americans

who intend to remain here become Catholics, to a man; the current phrase among them being,—"A man must leave his conscience at Cape Horn...."

The houses here, as everywhere else in California, are of one story, built of clay made into large bricks, about a foot and a half square and three or four inches thick, and hardened in the sun.... They have no chimneys or fire-places in the houses, the climate being such as to make a fire unnecessary; and all their cooking is done in a small cook-house, separated from the house. The Indians... do all the hard work, two or three being attached to each house; and the poorest persons are able to keep one, at least.[1]

Despite the fact that foreigners were viewed with suspicion by the Californians, growing numbers of Americans were settling on the West Coast in Dana's day, and they were prospering as traders and merchants. "By marrying natives, and bringing up their children as Catholics and Mexicans, and not teaching them the English language, they quiet suspicion, and even become popular and leading men," Dana noted.[2] Like many Americans of his day, he believed that his countrymen were by nature "more industrious and effective" than Mexicans. "In the hands of an enterprising people, what a country this might be!" he wrote.[3]

TEXAS

Americans were arriving in even greater numbers in another Mexican province, Texas. In 1821, Mexico granted Stephen Austin of Missouri permission to settle no more than 300 families on a section of Texas land that had been granted to his father. Soon, generous grants of land encouraged other agents, or *empresarios*, to bring more people. By 1835, about 20,000 new settlers, mostly Americans, were living in Texas, along with about 4,000 slaves. And friction was growing between them and the Mexican government.

Unlike the Americans who had settled in California by this date, the Texans kept strong ties to the United States. They did not convert to Catholicism or stop speaking English, although the Mexican government expected them to do so. And when Mexico abolished slavery in 1829—almost forty years before the United States—the Texans refused to give up the practice. They also objected to customs duties and other controls imposed by the government.

Many of the Texans were not set on independence at first, but their position hardened when Santa Anna made it clear that he would not negotiate a settlement to their demands. The Mexican government, for its part, was deeply suspicious of the Texans and believed that the United States had plans to take control of the province.

There was good reason for concern. Some Americans believed that Texas rightfully belonged to the United States, as part of Louisiana; when the United States had bought that huge territory from France in 1803, no one had been sure of its precise boundaries. The U.S. government hadn't claimed Texas, but it had offered to buy the province several times. And American settlers kept arriving, even when Mexico tried to stop the immigration.

In October 1835, a group of Texans formed a "war party" and took over the towns of Gonzales and San Antonio. Santa Anna promptly marched north with a large army to put down the uprising. On March 2, 1835, the Texans declared their independence and formed a provisional republic, with Sam Houston, formerly of Tennessee, heading its army. By then, Santa Anna's army had reached San Antonio and laid siege to the Alamo, a mission church where 187 rebels made a last stand. All were killed when the Alamo fell, on March 6. A week later, the rebels were hit with an even worse blow: At Goliad, Santa Anna's army captured and killed four hundred of their number.

The two defeats left Houston with fewer than four hundred soldiers. He retreated east, with the Mexican army in pursuit. New recruits joined him and soon brought his force back up to eight hundred. Santa Anna, meanwhile, made a fatal miscalculation. Believing that the rebellion had been crushed, he split his army into smaller units. When the rebels surprised what was left of his main force at San Jacinto, near present-day Houston, on April 21, they won a resounding victory. Santa Anna himself was captured and forced to give up the fight.

Across the border, Americans cheered the Texas rebellion. Houston was hailed as a hero, and Davy Crockett, James Bowie, and the other fighters at the Alamo instantly became legends. Santa Anna was portrayed in the press as a coward and a sneak.

Mexicans, not surprisingly, saw matters differently. The independence of Texas was a fact, but the Mexican government refused to recognize it. Specifically, Mexico warned that if Texas were to join the United States, Mexico would consider that reason to declare war on the United States.

Many Americans urged the U.S. government to annex Texas anyway, and Texas formally applied for admission. Stephen Austin wrote in support of annexation, saying that he had initially settled the region as a service to his native land. "If the U.S. let this opportunity pass to acquire Texas, it will be the greatest political error committed by that gov't since its existence," he warned.[4]

But, apart from not wanting to start a war with Mexico, the United States had reason to hesitate. The main problem was slavery, an issue that by 1836 had begun to tear the United States apart. Just sixteen years earlier, in 1820, opponents and supporters of slavery had reached a carefully crafted compromise that kept the number of slave states and free states equal, so that neither side would be able to control the U.S. Congress. Admitting Texas as a slave state could tip the balance—and Texas was so big that it could even be split into several slave states. Northerners balked.

Mexico watched the debate uneasily. Its concerns were only increased by a bizarre event in 1842: A U.S. Navy officer, wrongly believing that the United States and Mexico were at war, seized the town of Monterey, California. The United States promptly returned the town, but Mexico saw that California could easily go the way of Texas. And as the fact of Texas independence sank in, the Mexican government began to think that a free but weak Texas might be a better next-door neighbor than a Texas that was part of the United States, which seemed increasingly hungry for land. Britain and France, which had no wish to see the United States absorb more territory, encouraged this view and also offered aid to the Texans.

By 1845, Mexico was ready to recognize Texas as an independent nation. Partly to prevent this and to keep British and French influence out of the Southwest, the United States finally offered statehood. Texas entered the Union as the twenty-eighth state in December. Within five months, fighting broke out between Mexico and the United States.

WAR WITH MEXICO

A border dispute touched off war between the United States and Mexico in 1846, but the reasons for the conflict ran deeper. Despite the looming disagreement over slavery,

Americans in the mid-1800's were filled with extraordinary confidence and national pride. Many believed that the United States was fated to control all of North America. In July 1845, an article about the annexation of Texas in the *United States Magazine and Democratic Review* expressed this view with a phrase that would stick: "It is our manifest destiny to overspread the continent allotted by Providence for the free development of our multiplying millions," proclaimed the unsigned article, which was probably written by the New York magazine's editor, John L. O'Sullivan.[5]

"Manifest destiny" soon became a rallying cry for those who believed that the United States should expand all the way to the Pacific Ocean, taking in not just Texas but Oregon and California as well. Support for their view swelled just at the time when Mexico, independent for only twenty-five years, was struggling with debts and internal divisions. If the United States wanted to take Mexican territory, this surely was the moment.

Among the supporters of "manifest destiny" was James K. Polk, who in 1844 campaigned for the presidency and won the election on the issue of territorial expansion. He began negotiations with Great Britain that would eventually bring the Oregon Territory under U.S. control. Polk also wanted to buy California and New Mexico, but Mexico rejected the idea. Tensions between the two countries were growing so strong that negotiation seemed impossible. Texas statehood brought matters to a head.

When Texas joined the Union, its border with Mexico was unclear. Texans, in their declaration of independence, claimed land as far south as the Rio Grande; however, the Mexican state of Tamaulipas actually extended up to the Nueces River, which empties into the Gulf of Mexico about 150 miles north of the Rio Grande. But so few people lived in the arid strip of land between the rivers that neither side had bothered to make good on its claim.

Polk decided to press the issue. Early in 1846, he sent General Zachary Taylor across the Nueces and into the disputed territory, with orders to take up a position on the north bank of the Rio Grande. Mexicans considered this an invasion of their territory and, not willing to let the act go unchallenged, sent a cavalry unit across the Rio Grande. On April 24, the Mexican cavalry skirmished with a U.S. patrol, and eleven Americans were killed.

When news of the clash reached Polk in Washington, D.C., he sent a message to Congress demanding war. Mexico, he said, had "invaded our territory and shed American blood upon American soil."[6] Whether Polk was more interested in obtaining California than in avenging this clash or settling the Texas border issue is open to question—and many Americans (including a young congressman from Illinois, Abraham Lincoln) did question both the need to fight and the drive for expansion.

Theirs was a minority view, though, and Congress voted for war. In fact, when Polk's war message reached Congress on May 11, Taylor's army had already moved south into Mexican territory and won two battles, at Palo Alto and Resaca de la Palma. The Americans soon captured Matamoros, on the south side of the Rio Grande. U.S. ships blockaded Mexico's gulf ports, while Taylor paused to build up his forces. Then, with an army of about 5,000 men, he moved south, taking the Mexican city of Monterrey in September 1846.

Although Mexico had threatened war, it was unprepared. The Mexican government may have thought that American territorial demands would not lead to war, or that the United States would fight Britain over Oregon, giving Mexico a powerful ally. In any case, Mexico's army was in disarray, and it had no funds to pay for a war. Santa Anna, who had been forced from power and exiled, was hastily recalled. He talked Polk into granting him safe passage through the American blockade, promising to negotiate a peace that would favor U.S. interests. However, once in Mexico, he quickly raised an army of 20,000 men and marched to meet Taylor. They clashed at Buena Vista, near Monterrey, in February 1847. Although Santa Anna's force was larger, many of his soldiers were raw recruits, and they were tired from their long march. After two days of bitter fighting, he was forced to retreat. Taylor (nicknamed "Old Rough and Ready" by his troops for his casual dress and manners) was hailed as a hero. His success at Buena Vista would help him win election as president the next year.

Meanwhile, U.S. forces were moving on Mexican territory throughout the Southwest. Santa Fe was taken without a fight in August 1846, and all of New Mexico was soon under U.S. control. In California, the situation was more complicated. Native Californians were unhappy with Mexican rule, and U.S. officials hoped that they might join with American settlers to shake it off.

In June 1846, John C. Frémont, an army officer who had been sent to California on an exploring expedition, lit the spark for an uprising. He joined with a group of American settlers in the Sacramento Valley to proclaim California the independent "Bear Flag Republic." The new republic quickly voted to join the United States, and over the next few months, U.S. Navy ships secured coastal towns such as Monterey and San Francisco. But the native Californians were outraged by the creation of the new republic and rebelled, driving out the American forces. Finally the United States sent reinforcements by land, and California was under American control by early 1847.

Mexico was in no position to defend these territories—it

was dealing with an invasion far to the south. An American army under General Winfield Scott landed at Veracruz, on Mexico's gulf coast, in March 1847, and the city was in U. S. hands by the end of the month. Scott then turned his army west toward Mexico City, taking the route that the Spanish conqueror Hernán Cortés had used centuries earlier to advance on the Aztec capital.

Scott's force was outnumbered by the Mexican forces under Santa Anna, and it was made up mostly of volunteers. Attacking the capital struck some military experts as folly. However, the Americans were led by capable officers, many of whom (including Ulysses S. Grant and Robert E. Lee) would become famous in the U.S. Civil War. More important, they were better supplied and better armed than the Mexicans. They won important victories at Cerro Gordo and Puebla and then, after pausing for a few weeks, at Churubusco and Contreras. The Mexicans fought bravely and fiercely, but they were defeated each time. On September 12 and 13, the Americans captured Chapultepec Castle, overlooking Mexico City. This fortress served as Mexico's military academy, and among its defenders were thirteen- to fifteen-year-old cadets who fought valiantly, but fruitlessly, to their deaths.

One of those who fought on the American side at Chapultepec was Ulysses S. Grant, who described in his memoirs how he placed a howitzer on a church steeple overlooking the action. He was promoted to captain for his role in the battle.

> When I knocked for admission [to the church] a priest came to the door, who, while extremely polite, declined to admit us. With the little Spanish then at my command, I explained to him that he might save property by opening the door, and he certainly would save himself from becoming a prisoner, for a time

at least; and besides, I intended to go in whether he consented or not. He began to see his duty in the same light that I did, and opened the door, though he did not look as if it gave him special pleasure to do so. The gun was carried to the belfry and put together.... The shots from our little gun dropped in upon the enemy and created great confusion. Why they did not send out a small party and capture us, I do not know.[7]

Chapultepec was the last roadblock to Mexico City, and on September 14 the U. S. flag was raised over the National Palace in the heart of the capital. Santa Anna, who had fled south, tried to keep resistance alive, but the war was over. Mexico was forced to sue for peace.

Mexican resentment of the United States was high, and not only because American forces now occupied vast areas of Mexican territory. The U.S. volunteers were poorly disciplined, and there were reports of robbery, rape, and murder. General Scott himself, although he praised the conduct of his troops overall, acknowledged that some volunteers had "committed atrocities to make Heaven weep."[8] Back in the States, however, the soldiers and their officers were almost universally cheered as heroes. And many people, both in and out of the U.S. government, saw no reason to settle for California and the dry regions along the Rio Grande after the resounding victories the army had won. Why not annex all of Mexico?

NEW UNITED STATES TERRITORIES

In March 1847, at about the time that Scott was attacking Veracruz, Polk had sent a special minister to Mexico City with instructions to negotiate a treaty. Nicholas Trist, the envoy, had been told to obtain California and New Mexico—

nearly half of Mexico's total territory—in exchange for $30 million. Mexico had refused to negotiate, and Scott's military victories then put the United States in a strong position to demand more. Trist, however, ignored orders to return home and stayed in Mexico City. By early February 1848, he had concluded a treaty based on the original terms.

Southern Democrats were among those who urged Polk to reject this treaty and take more land. Some believed that the United States was destined to absorb all of Mexico. The call for annexation met strong opposition, however. Many Northerners feared that slavery might be extended into Mexico if it were absorbed. And Polk's political opponents saw increased demands for territory as proof that the president had started the war simply to grab land. Polk's diaries show that, while he was tempted to press for more territory, political realities led him to stick with his original demands. He reasoned that Mexico would be unlikely to agree to peace on stricter terms than Trist had offered. If that happened, the state of war would continue, and the U.S. Army would have to stay in Mexico—something that could give his political opponents ammunition to use against him:

> They [Polk's opponents] have falsely charged that the war was brought on and is continued by me with a view to the conquest of Mexico, and if I were now to reject a treaty made upon my own terms . . . the probability is that Congress would not grant either men or money to prosecute the war. Should this be the result, the army now in Mexico would be constantly wasting and diminishing in numbers, and I might at last be compelled to withdraw them, and then lose the two provinces of New Mexico and Upper California.[9]

With an eye to the upcoming presidential election, Polk sent the Treaty of Guadalupe-Hidalgo to the Senate, which approved a modified version on March 10, 1848. Under the final agreement, the United States received the New Mexico and California territories and paid Mexico $15 million, as well as assuming responsibility for about $3 million in claims that U.S. citizens had made against the Mexican government. Mexico at last accepted the U.S. annexation of Texas and recognized the Rio Grande as the border between the two countries. Polk lost the election anyway, but the country gained more than a half million square miles of land, roughly one-sixth of what is today the continental United States.

The impact on American history was enormous. As English-speaking settlers moved into the region in growing numbers, the culture changed. Mexicans were not pushed out in the same way that Native Americans were displaced elsewhere, but they were overwhelmed. They became, in effect, second-class citizens in an Anglo society. And the United States gained more than land for settlement. It won access to the Pacific Ocean (including what was probably the best port on North America's western coast, at San Francisco) and rich natural resources. Wealth from gold discovered in California in 1848, and from gold, silver, copper, and other minerals discovered there and in the Rockies in later years, went to the United States, not Mexico.

LAND FOR THE RAILROAD

Another chunk of Mexican territory passed to the United States in 1853. Now that the country stretched from the Atlantic to the Pacific, it needed better ways to move people and goods across the continent. Traveling by wagon across the plains, or by ship around the tip of South America, could take months. What was needed was a transcontinental railroad.

One of the proposed routes ran from New Orleans through Texas and New Mexico to California. There was just one problem: To take advantage of low mountain passes, the route ran south of the Gila River in Arizona, and under the Treaty of Guadalupe-Hidalgo, that was Mexican territory. In addition, disputes kept cropping up about the exact location of sections of the border. So, in 1853, President Franklin Pierce sent a leading advocate of the southern transcontinental route, railroad executive James Gadsden, to Mexico City as a United States minister, with instructions to buy a strip of territory. Pierce knew that the Mexican government was short of funds and was fighting an Indian uprising in the southeast, and he reasoned that it would be willing to sell. He was right.

In the Gadsden Purchase, concluded in 1854, the United States paid $10 million for just under 30,000 square miles of land that today form the southern parts of Arizona and New Mexico. Pierce had hoped to get Baja (Lower) California in the bargain, but the Mexican negotiators were so put off by Gadsden's swaggering manner that they refused to sell it.

Many Mexicans, still stinging from defeat in 1848, were livid that their government had sold even the border strip. Santa Anna's willingness to go along with the sale helped set off a revolt that once again drove him from power in 1855.

An odd footnote to the border issue was provided by William Walker, an adventurer from Tennessee. Onetime doctor, lawyer, and journalist, Walker was a short, slight man with piercing gray eyes and enormous ambitions. In 1853 he invaded Baja California with a private armed force, landing at La Paz and declaring an independent republic with himself as president.

The Mexicans were, not surprisingly, hostile, and the United States blocked his supplies. He was forced to return to the United States, where he was tried for violating neutrality laws but acquitted.

Walker went on to continue his filibustering, as such adventures were called, in Central America; he died in front of a Honduran firing squad in 1860. Friction along the United States–Mexican border would continue far longer.

Benito Juárez (upper left), *Pancho Villa* (lower left), and *Emiliano Zapata* (right). Each played an important role in the development of Mexico as a nation.

3

REVOLUTION, INTERVENTION

"Poor Mexico! So far from God and so close to the United States."[1] That telling remark is credited to Porfirio Díaz, the dictator who held power in Mexico from the late 1800s through the early 1900s. Díaz's iron rule covered much of an era that was marked by turmoil and civil war. Territorial issues were settled, but tensions with the United States flared repeatedly. In both countries, events led people to form attitudes that can still be seen at work in relations between the countries.

In the late 1850s, at the start of this period, the border was fixed more or less where it is today. But it was far from peaceful. The rough, thinly populated country made an ideal base for bandits, adventurers, revolutionaries, and desperadoes of all stripes. Raids across the Rio Grande—in both directions—were common. So were tensions between Anglos (English speakers) and Mexicans in the territories the United States had so recently acquired from Mexico.

BORDER TROUBLES

Slavery, the issue that was dividing the United States, contributed to those tensions in Texas. While the network known as the Underground Railroad was helping slaves flee north from many Southern states, a significant number of Texas slaves reached freedom by heading south to Mexico. Texas slave owners believed that Mexicans, who opposed slavery, were helping them. In 1856, Texans uncovered a plan for a slave revolt in south-central Texas, in which Mexicans were to help slaves kill their masters and escape over the border. Mexicans were driven out of the region, and Anglos at Goliad passed a resolution stating that "the continuance of the greaser or peon Mexicans as citizens among us is an intolerable nuisance and a grievance which calls loudly for redress."[2]

Friction developed over other issues as well. In the Texas Cart War, which broke out in 1857, Anglo bandits attacked the profitable Mexican-run oxcart wagon trains that carried freight between San Antonio and points south. Mexican raiders preyed on Anglo communities, too. One of the most flamboyant raiders was Juan Nepomuceno Cortina, known as the Red Robber of the Rio Grande (for his red hair). Starting in 1859, Cortina's band plagued the border for fifteen years, successfully eluding both United States and Mexican authorities.

Beyond the border region, however, neither Americans nor Mexicans paid much attention to these conflicts. Both countries were increasingly absorbed with internal problems. In 1861, the United States Civil War broke out. Mexico, meanwhile, was struggling through a period of revolution, reform, and foreign invasion.

REFORM AND OCCUPATION

After Santa Anna was driven from power in 1855, a group of young liberals set about remaking Mexican society. Led by Benito Juárez, a Zapotec Indian lawyer who would become one of Mexico's greatest national heroes, they tried to break the traditional power of the Church and the army. Church lands were confiscated, and special privileges enjoyed by the clergy and army were abolished. The reforms fell short of addressing some of the major underlying social inequalities that had existed since the days of Spanish rule. Juárez and other Liberals supported land reform in principle, for example, but they took no steps to break up large estates (haciendas) or distribute land to peasants because they needed the support of wealthy landowners. Nevertheless, their movement, known as La Reforma, led to a series of civil wars. By 1861, Juárez had emerged victorious, but the country was nearly bankrupt. Mexico was unable to make payments on its foreign debts. As a result, England, France, and Spain jointly invaded Mexico in 1862, with the goal of occupying the customs house at the port of Veracruz and controlling the stream of income it produced.

England and Spain soon withdrew, but France turned out to have grander goals. The French Emperor Napoleon III was bent on conquest, and his forces soon marched inland from Veracruz. The Mexicans delivered a stunning defeat to a French army at Puebla on May 5, 1862, an event celebrated today on the Mexican national holiday Cinco de Mayo. But the French regrouped and pressed on. In 1863, they captured Mexico City. Juárez was driven north to the border region, where he continued to fight. Another guerrilla army, led by Porfirio Díaz, fought the French in the south. But France controlled most of the country, and Napoleon III established a monarchy to govern it, placing Archduke Maximilian of Austria on the throne in 1864.

In the United States, people watched these events with growing unease. For more than forty years, the U.S. government had opposed any effort by European powers to expand their holdings in the Western Hemisphere. That policy was first set out by President James Monroe in 1823; in the 1840s, Polk had extended the Monroe Doctrine to bar even diplomatic interference by Europeans in the hemisphere. In fact, though, the policy had never really been put to the test. And as long as the United States was embroiled in a civil war, France felt free to ignore it.

That changed with the end of the United States Civil War, in 1865. When Union General Ulysses S. Grant accepted the surrender of Confederate General Robert E. Lee at Appomattox Court House in Virginia, the United States was able to turn its attention abroad—and it had a huge standing army, geared up for fighting, at its disposal. The U.S. government told France to give up its dreams of an empire in America and to leave Mexico. It backed up the demand by sending a sizable force to the Mexican border and beginning to supply Juárez with the modern weapons that had helped the North win the war. France reviewed the situation and pulled its forces out late in 1866, leaving Maximilian supported only by a small force of Mexican conservatives who opposed Juárez and other Liberals. The Mexican guerrilla forces attacked, and Maximilian was captured in May 1867. He was executed by a firing squad, and Juárez returned to power.

Mexico sorely needed peace—years of war had left its economy in shreds. Rebuilding began under Juárez, who died in office in 1872. Four years later Porfirio Díaz took power, driving Juárez's successor into exile, and promptly set about converting the Mexican republic to a dictatorship. Through a masterful blend of diplomacy, deceit, political finesse, corruption, and force, Díaz would hold power for thirty-four years, a period known as the Porfiriato. One of his first tasks was to bring peace to the border region, where friction with the United States was threatening to start yet another war.

As the United States had expanded westward, the wild, thinly populated Mexican border regions had become one of the last refuges of the Indians who were being pushed off their ancestral lands by white settlers. The international boundary meant little to Native Americans, except as a marker that helped them escape the authorities of both countries. Apaches, Kickapoos, Seminoles, and other groups lived along the border and raided on both sides of it, slipping across the boundary to elude capture. Frustrated soldiers of both countries often pursued them anyway, and that sparked several incidents. In 1873, for example, the U.S. cavalry chased a band of Kickapoo raiders into Mexico from Texas and destroyed their village. Mexico was outraged at this invasion of its territory, but the incident was not the last. When the United States proposed an agreement that would allow forces from either country to cross the border in pursuit of bandits and raiders, Mexicans suspected that the Americans were really after more territory. They refused.

The U.S. response provoked outrage south of the border. In 1877, the U.S. secretary of war formally instructed army leaders to cross the Rio Grande in pursuit of raiders whether or not Mexican authorities agreed, "to overtake and punish them, as well as retake stolen property taken from our citizens and found in their hands on the Mexican side of the line." A Mexican newspaper called the order an "offense to the national dignity, and to the sovereignty and independence of Mexico," and some Mexicans urged their government to send an army north in response.³

Fortunately, cooler heads prevailed. American diplomats recognized that the high-handed approach of the War Department's order had deeply insulted Mexico, and they worked to smooth relations. Mexicans, increasingly plagued by Apache raids, recognized the advantage of working alongside the United States to end the trouble. In 1885 Mexican-United States cooperation succeeded in ending the Chiricahua Apache uprising led by Geronimo, the last major Indian conflict along the border.

AMERICANS INVEST

As border troubles waned, the focus of relations between the United States and Mexico gradually changed. One of Díaz's main goals was to move Mexico into the twentieth century as a modern, industrial state. He was helped by a group of officials called *cientificos*, who systematically revised tax and trade laws, reorganized the government's finances, and generally created an attractive climate for foreign investors. With political stability ensured by Díaz's firm grip on power and the economy at last looking up, U.S. investors in particular began to look south for opportunities. U.S. firms laid thousands of miles of railroad track linking rural areas of Mexico to cities and ports so that raw materials could be moved out of the interior. They also expanded Mexico's mining industry and, by the beginning of the twentieth century, began to pump oil from rich reserves discovered in eastern Mexico.

By 1910 American investment in Mexico totaled more than $1 billion, and U.S. firms controlled half of Mexico's oil and three-fourths of its other minerals. Americans also owned huge plantations and cattle ranches in Mexico. As much as a fifth of Mexico's farmland came under the control of foreign land companies, many based in the United States, which then resold the land to would-be ranchers and plantation owners in America and elsewhere.[4]

Not surprisingly, American business interests strongly supported Díaz, despite the corruption and inequality that marked his regime. The dictator was viewed as Mexico's savior by some people north of the border; one magazine reporter, for example, praised him as the "hero of modern Mexico."[5] But even Díaz grew uneasy as the extent of American investment increased, and he began to encourage British and French firms to become more involved.

In fact, while Mexico gained much from the investment, the benefits were mixed at best. Most of the new wealth pouring into the country went to government officials and the elite. Workers and small farmers—mainly Indians and *mestizos* (people of mixed Indian and Spanish ancestry)—actually lost ground during the Porfiriato. Miners and other laborers worked long hours for low wages; if they tried to organize unions, they were fired. In the early 1900s, the government brutally crushed strikes at mines and textile mills.

Meanwhile, under new land laws, peasants lost rights to the small plots of land that in many cases their families had worked for generations. When Yaqui Indians rebelled in protest over the sale of their land to foreigners, the United States sent troops to help end the rebellion. Mexicans who protested such actions were arrested; many were "shot while attempting to escape" by the *rurales*, the police who were supposed to keep law and order in the countryside but were often no more than outlaws in uniforms. Some of the government's most vocal critics, including the brothers Enrique, Ricardo, and Jesús Flores Magón, fled across the border to the United States, where they continued to speak out against the Díaz regime.

The events that would finally sweep Díaz from power began in 1910. Although he suppressed political parties and firmly controlled elections, the dictator repeatedly asserted that he would step down if Mexicans elected another leader. Francisco Madero, the son of a wealthy landowner, took him at his word and decided to oppose him in the election of 1910. He was a political novice and, as a member of the country's elite, an unlikely revolutionary, but his campaign sparked enormous enthusiasm. There was virtually no way that Madero could win (Díaz controlled the vote counting), but the dictator was alarmed all the same. Madero was arrested on a trumped-up charge and held in jail until the election. When he was finally released on bail, he fled north, disguising himself as a railroad mechanic to cross the border by train. From a base in San Antonio, he began to plot rebellion.

REVOLUTION

Madero's uprising began on November 20, 1910. He recrossed the border while, by arrangement, small bands of his supporters took up arms in many parts of Mexico. The government quickly put out these little brushfires, and Madero was forced to flee back to Texas. But the action inspired others, and the revolution continued. In the north, former bandits and cowboys were encouraged by Madero's action to form guerrilla bands that attacked the Díaz forces and raided big estates.

Among their leaders were Abraham Gonzales, Pascual Orozco, and Doroteo Arango—who would become famous under the alias Francisco (Pancho) Villa. Villa, who had grown up as a peasant on a hacienda, was a bandit and cattle rustler, but he already had a glowing reputation. An American journalist who traveled with his army wrote:

His reckless and romantic bravery is the subject of countless poems. They tell, for example, how one of his band named Reza was captured by the *rurales* and bribed to betray Villa. Villa heard of it and sent word into the city of Chihuahua that he was coming for Reza. In broad daylight he entered the city on horse-back, took ice cream in the Plaza—the ballad is very explicit on this point—and rode up and down the streets until he found Reza strolling with his sweetheart in the Sunday crowd on the Paseo Bolivar, where he shot him and escaped. In time of famine he fed whole districts, and took care of entire villages evicted by the soldiers under Porfirio Díaz's outrageous land law. Everywhere he was known as the Friend of the Poor. He was the Mexican Robin Hood.[6]

The guerrillas began to score victories against the government troops, and in February 1911, Madero reentered Mexico to join Orozco and Villa. Their forces captured the border city of Ciudad Juárez in May. It was an odd alliance—Madero, the reluctant upper-class revolutionary who preferred negotiation to battle, paired with a former mule skinner and a onetime bandit who would rather settle matters with a bullet—but it worked for a time. Their success encouraged other revolutionaries, including Emiliano Zapata, a champion of land reform who led an Indian army against the Díaz forces. By the end of May, Díaz had been forced to resign and had fled to exile in Europe. Madero was elected president the following October, but Mexico's troubles were far from over.

For Zapata, the gradual pace of reform proposed by Madero was far too slow. Zapata wanted restoration of the lands taken from peasants during the Porfiriato, plus confiscation of a third of the holdings of wealthy landowners, and he refused to lay down arms. Madero also angered Orozco by failing to give him a major government post, so he soon faced rebellion on two fronts. He sent General Victoriano Huerta to subdue the Zapatistas, without much success, and against Orozco, who was forced into Arizona. But Huerta then joined forces with former supporters of Díaz, conservatives for whom any reform was too much. In 1913, with their support, Huerta overthrew Madero, who was arrested and then killed, allegedly while "attempting to escape."

The United States was officially neutral in the conflict between Díaz and Madero, but it was not entirely an idle spectator. Under President William Howard Taft, the United States recognized Madero as Mexico's elected president. But American investors longed for the return of the Díaz days, and they found a supporter in the U.S. ambassador to Mexico, Henry Lane Wilson. Wilson urged the U.S. government to oppose Madero and, when he could not convince his superiors on that point, joined in the plot that brought Huerta to power. By that time, however, the United States had a new president—Woodrow Wilson—who categorically refused to recognize Huerta's bloody coup. Ambassador Wilson was forced to resign.

Huerta's rule was as brutal as his rise to power, and he spent most of it (when he was not drunk) battling rebellions in the south, led by Zapata, and in the north, led by Villa, Venustiano Carranza, and others. As his opponents gradually closed in on him, he also faced growing animosity from the United States. Not long after taking office in 1913, President Wilson sent a personal representative to Huerta to offer "counsel and assistance" in working out a settlement. Wilson proposed an immediate cease-fire, followed by a free and fair election, in which Huerta would not be a candidate. Huerta rejected the plan. That led Wilson, in a speech to a joint session of Congress, to outline his thoughts on what he called "the deplorable posture of affairs" in Mexico:

The peace, prosperity, and contentment of Mexico mean more, much more, to us than merely an enlarged field of our commerce and enterprise. They mean an enlargement of the field of self-government and the realization of the hopes and rights of a nation with whose best aspirations, so long suppressed and disappointed, we deeply sympathize. We shall yet prove to the Mexican people that we know how to serve them without first thinking how we shall serve ourselves.[7]

Wilson speculated that his peace plan had been rejected because Huerta "did not realize the spirit of the American people in this matter" and "did not believe that the present administration spoke . . . for the people of the United States." The Mexican leader might have been excused for some confusion. Wilson's well-intentioned and high-minded (if somewhat high-handed) approach was a radical departure from the views of the U.S. investors Huerta was familiar with, and whose interests he had made it a point to support.

American business interests were angered by Wilson's policy, and European powers were bemused. But many Americans shared Wilson's view of the Mexican conflict. They abhorred Huerta's violence and sympathized with Carranza, a liberal landowner who favored moderate political reform and constitutional democracy. And even though Villa had been a cattle rustler and bandit for twenty years before taking up the revolutionary cause, they still viewed him as a dashing and romantic figure.

Wilson soon turned his thoughts into action. In 1912, the United States had barred sales of weapons and ammunition to all parties in the Mexican civil conflict. Wilson lifted the arms embargo early in 1914, believing that this would help Carranza and Villa. In fact, the rebels had been able to smuggle plenty of arms all along, and Huerta was more likely to benefit from the end of the embargo.

Huerta was getting most of his arms through the port of Veracruz, and in April 1914, the U.S. Marines invaded that port. The official reason was the arrest of several American sailors by authorities in the port of Tampico, who had quickly realized their mistake and released the men. The underlying reasons had more to do with the Mexican civil war. The invasion disrupted arms shipments to Huerta and forced him to send troops to defend the city, withdrawing them from the fight against the rebels. It thus helped bring about his downfall. But even the rebels condemned the action as a violation of Mexican sovereignty.

Huerta fled the country in July, but fighting continued, with Villa and Carranza battling each other for control of Mexico. After a year of near total lawlessness and some of the bloodiest battles ever fought on Mexican soil, Carranza controlled most of the country and was recognized by the United States as its legitimate president. Villa was driven north, to his base in Chihuahua. And once again, conflict erupted along the border.

VILLA AT THE BORDER

Beginning in 1915, a series of border raids by Mexican outlaw groups fanned fears and tensions between Anglos and Mexicans. Many of these raids were prompted by a bizarre plot, called the Plan of San Diego, to foment a racial war in the border region. The mostly Mexican conspirators hoped to drive Anglos out of the Southwest and retake the territories lost earlier in the Mexican War. By mid-1916, more than thirty Americans had been killed in roughly twenty-five such raids.

However, the man behind the most serious attacks was not part of the Plan of San Diego. Pancho Villa's full motives may never be known, but he deeply resented the fact that the

United States had recognized Carranza, believing that this was at least partly responsible for his failure to win the Mexican civil war. International politics may also have played a role in both Villa's raids and the Plan of San Diego. After World War I broke out in Europe in 1914, German agents actively fomented trouble between Mexico and the United States, hoping to keep the United States out of the European war by involving it in conflict with its neighbor.

On January 10, 1916, a band of Villistas attacked a train that was carrying a group of eighteen American miners, who were traveling (supposedly under government protection) to a mine in Chihuahua. At Santa Ysabel, a cattle station on the Mexican side of the border, the American miners were taken off the train and shot in cold blood by Villa's raiders. The Santa Ysabel Massacre, as the U.S. press called the action, shocked Americans and ended any support Villa might once have enjoyed in the United States.

Villa was already planning an even bolder action. On March 9, he attacked the town of Columbus, New Mexico, with a force of nearly five hundred men. The raiders robbed a bank (which, according to some accounts, Villa believed owed him money) and several other businesses, killed nine soldiers and eight civilians, burned a hotel, and then made for the border with the U.S. cavalry in hot pursuit.

The next day, General John J. Pershing was ordered to lead a military force into Mexico to end the threat from the Villistas and to capture their leader, dead or alive. Army units also crossed the Rio Grande to take action against other outlaw groups. Pershing's 4,000-man column effectively scattered Villa's forces but failed to catch Villa himself.

For months, the Americans, bolstered by reinforcements, pursued the revolutionary leader deep into Mexican territory. The farther they went and the longer they stayed, the stronger the resistance they met. The Carranza government, which at first agreed to the action, began to protest. U.S. Secretary of State Robert Lansing wrote a sharp reply that catalogued the wrongs done by Mexican raiders and the Mexican government's failure to stop them:

> American garrisons have been attacked at night, American soldiers killed, and their equipment and horses stolen. American ranches have been raided, property stolen and American trains wrecked and plundered.... In these attacks on American territory, Carranzita adherents and even Carranzita soldiers took part in the looting and killing.... Leaders of the bandits well known both to Mexican civil and military authorities, as well as to American officers, have been enjoying with impunity the liberty of the towns of Northern Mexico. So far has the indifference of the [Mexican] Government to these atrocities gone that some of these leaders, as I am told, have received not only the protection of that Government, but encouragement and aid.[8]

Pershing's forces never did catch Villa, and they finally withdrew in February 1917, when the United States was on the brink of entering World War I.

In an odd twist, Mexico was involved in the events that brought the United States into that war. In January, the U.S. government obtained a copy of a secret telegram from the German foreign secretary, Alfred Zimmerman, to the German envoy in Mexico City. It revealed that Germany intended to start all-out submarine warfare against shipping in the Atlantic Ocean, and it proposed that if this brought the United States into the war on the Allied side, Mexico should come in on the German side. "We shall give general financial support, and it is understood that Mexico is to reconquer the lost territory in New Mexico, Texas and Arizona," Zimmerman wrote.[9]

German submarine attacks began in February, and the United States declared war on April 6. Mexico stayed out. But Mexico saw no peace—civil war continued. Zapata rose up against Carranza in the south, saying that the president had taken over large estates not to redistribute land but to benefit his supporters. "A group of friends are helping you enjoy the spoils of war: wealth, honors, business deals, banquets, luxurious and licentious feasts, drunken carousing, orgies of ambition, of power and of blood," Zapata wrote in an open letter to Carranza. "The hopes of the people have been turned to scorn."[10]

Carranza personally arranged for Zapata's assassination in 1919. He was assassinated himself the next year. Altogether, one million Mexicans died in the fighting that tore the country apart from 1910 to 1920.

MEXICO'S OIL

Carranza's greatest accomplishment was the constitution of 1917. It set up a federal republic and contained key provisions that limited presidents to one term, guaranteed public education, gave workers the right to strike, and restricted the power of the Church. In terms of relations with the United States, however, the most important provision was Article 27, which involved the ownership of land. The new constitution embraced the principle of land reform, giving the government the power to confiscate and redistribute land when doing so served national interests. Subsoil mineral rights were held to belong to the nation. American investors, and especially American oil companies, were alarmed. Some demanded that the United States invade Mexico immediately. But Carranza did not really enforce the provision, and the matter rested for the balance of his time in power.

The situation changed when Carranza's successor, General Alvaro Obregón, took office. The son of a rancher who had slipped into poverty, Obregón had been allied with Carranza through much of the civil war. Perhaps because he had worked in many different jobs as a young man, he had great sympathy for workers and others on the low rungs of Mexican society. He was determined to improve their lot, and he set about implementing the constitution of 1917. The American oil companies had powerful friends in Washington, including Secretary of the Interior Albert B. Fall (who would eventually go to jail for his role in the Teapot Dome affair, a scheme in which oil companies illegally obtained drilling rights on federal land). Because of their pressure, the United States refused to recognize the Obregón government for three years, until Obregón agreed not to apply Article 27 to land where the oil companies had been drilling before 1917.

Obregón was a great compromiser, and he successfully smoothed over this and many other disputes. He was followed by a series of presidents, all handpicked by leaders of the ruling party, who redistributed millions of acres of farmland from wealthy landowners to peasants and small farmers. Mexico at last seemed on the road to stability—but business interests in the United States did not see it that way. They viewed the reforms as socialism (government control of the economy), pure and simple, and called repeatedly for intervention. A 1920s newspaper editorial gave voice to this view:

> There will never be a stable government in Mexico until the United States imposes one and sustains it with . . . American bayonets. . . . There is no human power anywhere that can reestablish order in that unhappy country except the power of the United States of America. Early or later, our government must do what the Hearst newspapers for three years have suggested it do: Intervene in Mexico energetically, dignifiedly, and in suf-

ficient force, not in order to suppress the Mexican people but to save them.[11]

The arrogance of such statements was reflected as well by the oil companies, who felt free to flout Mexican laws and drill wells without permits, drawing out oil at such an excessive rate that oil fields began to dry up and production levels plummeted. Finally, in 1938, a strike by oil workers brought matters to a head. When the oil companies didn't listen to the workers' demands, Mexican President Lázaro Cárdenas invoked Article 27 and took over the wells. The oil companies clamored for help from the U.S. government, demanding intervention. But President Franklin D. Roosevelt chose compromise instead. The two countries worked out a settlement under which the oil companies were paid $42 million (an amount far less than they believed they were owed), and Mexico's oil was at last in Mexican hands.

Roosevelt's response to the nationalization of the Mexican oil industry marked a major change in United States policy toward its neighbor to the south. But a century of friction—marked by conquest, border conflicts, intervention, and economic exploitation—had left attitudes that would prove more difficult to change. People in both countries tended to view each other in terms of unfair stereotypes. To many Americans, Mexicans were backward revolutionaries and bandits who needed to be "saved." To many Mexicans, Americans were "gringos"—rich, brash, arrogant, and domineering. These views would continue to color relations between the two countries.

Legal immigrants from Mexico enter the United States at busy border crossings such as this one.

4

THE MIGRANTS

The United States–Mexican border is one of the longest in the world between a wealthy nation and a developing country. And ever since the second half of the nineteenth century, when the border was fixed and the settlement of the American West began to open up new opportunities, it has been porous. Millions of Mexicans have crossed it in search of work, some to stay only temporarily in the United States, others to remain.

The tide of migration has risen and fallen over the years, depending on economic factors in both countries. At different times the United States has encouraged migrants from Mexico or has tried to block their entry, and Mexican workers have found prejudice and resentment, as well as work, north of the border. To Mexicans, the flow across the border represents both a great opportunity and a symptom of trouble at home, because it highlights their country's own economic difficulties. To people in the United States, migration from Mexico is both a problem and a solution to other problems. Often, it has also been a convenient scapegoat for complex economic and social issues that defy quick fixes.

CONTROVERSY

People in the United States have almost always held conflicting views about immigrants—not only immigrants from Mexico, but immigrants from practically anywhere. For more than a century after independence, most Americans shared the view that the country could and perhaps should absorb almost limitless numbers of people from abroad. There was always more land to the west for settlement and expansion. But even in the early days, immigration was controversial. Benjamin Franklin, for example, worried that German settlers weren't "English" enough for the new United States.

The United States did not start to keep records on immigration until the 1820s. In that decade, about 140,000 immigrants arrived. More than four times as many came in the 1830s, and in the 1840s more than one million. That marked the start of a great wave of immigration that would bring more than nine million people to the United States by the end of the 1870s.

The new arrivals came mainly from English-speaking countries—England, Canada, Ireland—and from northern European countries such as Germany. Their decision to leave their homes behind and try their luck in America was sparked partly by troubles in their home countries, such as the potato-crop failures and famine that swept Ireland in the 1840s, and partly by encouragement from the United States. American officials who dreamed of manifest destiny realized that to settle and hold the vast western lands, the United States needed many more people. Railroads also encouraged immigrants; more people farming and living in the West meant more goods being shipped by rail, and more profits. Railroad companies circulated pamphlets and broadsides extolling the virtues of America, and some sent recruiters abroad to urge Europeans to make the trip.

The immigrants of the mid-1800s looked and for the most part sounded like the Americans of the day—who, after all, were the children and grandchildren of earlier immigrants from Europe—and they shared many of the same customs. They thus blended easily into U.S. society.

Nonetheless, as the numbers of immigrants increased, so did resentment against them. Immigrants, who were often willing to work at menial jobs for low wages, were accused of taking jobs from American workers. The Irish were singled out for their Catholicism; Germans and Scandinavians, for their languages. This was the first appearance of nativism—the belief that people born on American soil were somehow better, and entitled to more, than people born elsewhere.

The best-known adherents of the nativist view were the Know-Nothings, members of various semisecret societies who opposed immigration but, when asked about their activities, always responded, "I don't know." These people eventually formed the American, or Know-Nothing, Party, which polled large votes in the mid-1850s. Still, theirs was a minority view. The Know-Nothings split over the issue of slavery, and their party dissolved after the election of 1856.

THE GOLDEN DOOR?

Nativism wasn't dead, however. It resurfaced in the late 1800s and early 1900s, which saw another great wave of immigration. Once again, Americans struggled with conflicting views—welcoming immigrants on the one hand, resenting them on the other.

The spirit of welcome had taken concrete form in the Statue of Liberty, described (in the poem by Emma Lazarus carved at the statue's base) as lifting a lamp to light the way to a "golden door" of opportunity in America. But by 1910, nearly 15 percent of the U.S. population was foreign born, an all-time high. This time, many of the immigrants came from eastern and southern Europe and (especially in California) from Asia. They looked and sounded different from native-born Americans, and they followed different customs. That increased resentment, and racism also began to color American views of immigration.

Ever since the 1840s, when the Mexican War brought California and the Southwest under the U.S. flag, small numbers of Mexicans had been among the immigrants to the United States. When the territory changed hands, political borders changed, but cultural change was much slower. Mexicans who lived south of the new international border still had family and business ties with Mexicans to the north, so some movement across the border was to be expected.

It was during the late 1800s, however, that Mexican immigrants first began to arrive in large numbers. Agriculture was growing rapidly in the West, and farms and ranches needed workers. So did railroads, which had thousands of miles of new routes to maintain. The wave of Mexican immigration that began in the late 1800s peaked between 1910 and 1930, when between 500,000 and 800,000 Mexicans went north in search of work. U.S. labor needs during World War I and the booming 1920s encouraged many to make the trip. So did the long and bloody civil war in Mexico, which forced thousands of people to leave their homes.

NOW WE WANT YOU, NOW WE DON'T

For many Mexican immigrants at the turn of the century, crossing the border was not a major step. In their parents' day, the border region had been part of Mexico, and it still had an informal culture of its own, with family, social, and economic links that ignored the international boundary. Until the U.S. Border Patrol was formed to police immigration in 1924, many immigrants just walked across unchallenged, and many Mexican workers moved back and forth between the two countries at will. Even when the United States began to patrol for illegal immigrants, there was no effort to limit legal immigration from Mexico—farmers wanted Mexican field workers, who would often work for half the wages demanded by Anglo workers.

That changed, however, during the Great Depression of the 1930s. Employment was scarce on both sides of the border; there was less reason for Mexicans to go north. Moreover, Mexicans were facing growing prejudice and discrimination in the United States.

Hard times often cause prejudice to intensify, because people find it easier to blame outsiders for their troubles than to struggle with the true causes, which are often rooted in hard-to-solve economic and social problems. And Mexicans were an easy target for prejudice in U.S. society, with its long history of racist undercurrents. *Mestizos*, with their Indian and Spanish heritage, were perceived from the start as racially different. Besides, unlike many other immigrants, Mexicans often did not rush to adopt American ways. They didn't really need to—they were able to maintain ties to their homeland and even return there frequently. They also found large communities of Spanish-speaking Mexican Americans firmly established in the United States when they arrived. As a result, they had less need to speak English or to give up the customs they were used to following. That fueled prejudice against them; Mexicans were seen as ignorant and lazy for not taking up the language and ways of the United States.

When the Depression made jobs of any kind few and far between, prejudice helped decide who got work. Many employers refused to hire any but white American workers. Undocumented Mexican immigrants—given the negative label "wetbacks" because many reached the United States by wading across the Rio Grande—were deported, and many other Mexicans decided to leave on their own. In all about 400,000 returned to Mexico. Even Mexican Americans who had been born in the United States faced prejudice and were treated like foreigners.

The cycle of now-we-want-you, now-we-don't would soon be repeated. The United States' entry into World War II in December 1941 once again created an enormous demand for labor. Americans left their jobs to join the armed forces, but there were crops to plant and harvest and factories to run, many of them making essential war supplies. American women entered the workforce in large numbers to meet the need, but the United States also looked abroad.

THE BRACERO PROGRAM

In 1942, the government established the Bracero Program, which brought contract workers (*braceros*) into the country for limited periods of time. Illegal immigration also picked up, and Mexican workers were generally welcomed whether they had work permits or not. Then, after the war, the government cracked down on illegal immigrants, rounding up Mexicans in groups and sending them back across the border. In 1954, the peak year of this policy, more than one million Mexicans were returned to their homeland.

The Bracero Program continued for another decade because western farmers had grown to depend on the cheap labor the program provided. By the time it ended, however, Mexican-American farmworkers were no longer willing to put up with low pay and substandard working conditions. In 1965, Mexican-American labor leader Cesar Chavez led migrant farmworkers in a successful strike against California grape growers. That action inspired other Mexican Americans to organize to demand fair pay, decent working conditions, and an end to discrimination. What became known as the Chicano movement (probably from the Spanish word *mejicano*, meaning "Mexican") swept the West. The movement helped end some abuses, but it gradually petered out.

One result of these contradictory immigration policies was a firm tradition among Mexicans of working in the United States for a period of time—usually several months, but sometimes a few years—and then returning home, in a regularly repeating cycle. The pattern filled needs on both sides of the border, giving employers in the United States a flexible and low-cost workforce and giving Mexican workers a way to funnel income to their families at home. As the tradition continued, however, it would help fuel friction between the two countries.

A NEW NATIVISM

The number of Mexicans traveling north across the border rose through the 1970s and 1980s, but estimates of just how many there were varied widely because the number of illegal migrants couldn't be accurately estimated. One yardstick was the number of undocumented migrants detained and returned by the border patrol each year; that number rose from just over 275,000 in 1970 to more than one million in 1983.[1] But those figures reflected tighter enforcement, not just more migrants. Perhaps more important, the figures reflected the number of detentions, not the number of people trying to enter the country without papers. Many Mexicans who were detained and sent back home promptly turned around and tried to enter the United States again, so some were certainly caught and counted more than once.

Who were these migrants? A study conducted by the Mexican government in the late 1970s showed that the overwhelming majority were men between the ages of fifteen and forty. Ninety percent were from northern Mexico, and on the whole they had more education than the national average. Nearly all had jobs in Mexico before they went north. Based on the results of this study, Mexican officials estimated that only a little over half of the workers who regularly traveled across the border to find work were in the United States at any given time. At the time, that was roughly 900,000 individuals.[2]

In the early 1980s, other studies showed that most of the workers stayed for six months or less. An average of 150,000 a year stayed longer, many becoming in effect permanent U.S. residents. They joined a population of Mexican origin and descent that was then about 10 million.[3]

When the Mexican study was done, U.S. estimates of the number of illegal aliens were far higher. One put the number of illegals from all countries at 12 million. A special government commission set up to study the problem came up with a lower figure; it estimated that there were between 3 and 6 million illegal immigrants in 1981. At the time, the United States was entering an economic recession, and these undocumented workers were seen as a threat—taking jobs from American workers, drawing on social services that were paid for by American taxpayers.

Growing resentment helped produce a backlash against

immigrants in general and, in southern California and parts of the Southwest, against immigrants from Mexico in particular. The porous United States–Mexican border had become a point of entry not only for Mexican workers but for refugees from the civil wars and political turmoil that swept through Central America in the 1980s. Most of these refugees were not granted political asylum, a status that would have allowed them to remain legally in the United States; but many stayed anyway. Especially in California, the 1970s and 1980s also saw an increase in immigration from Asia.

States that received the heaviest influx of immigrants found that they were faced with new problems, many of them rooted in language differences. Immigrants and the children of immigrants often didn't speak English, so schools needed to develop bilingual education programs that would allow students to keep learning in their native language as they became proficient in English. Government forms, voting materials, sometimes even signs were printed in two languages. And because many new immigrants were poor when they arrived and had trouble finding anything but low-paying jobs, large numbers were forced to turn to social services for assistance. That put a financial burden on states such as California, which received many immigrants.

A NEW LAW

In California and the Southwest, another concern soon emerged: Conservatives began to worry that growing immigration from Mexico would somehow overwhelm U.S. culture, supplanting it with a Spanish-speaking one. This concern grew in spite of evidence that young Mexican Americans were in fact increasingly blending into American society—marrying outside their ethnic group, for example, at twice the rate that their parents had.[4] It also ignored the fact that a Spanish-speaking Mexican society had existed in these regions long before they became part of the United States.

The fear that immigration would erode American society led to efforts to end or limit bilingual education in schools and eliminate Spanish-language voting materials, and to deny social services, including education, to undocumented workers and their children. These efforts were largely unsuccessful, but labor groups and even some Mexican Americans joined the chorus of concern over illegal immigration. Undocumented workers, they said, were willing to work for low pay; if they did not actually take the jobs of American workers, they pushed wages down. Because of their illegal status, they were also often mistreated by unscrupulous employers, who sometimes forced the immigrants to work in appalling conditions.

What finally emerged from the flurry of concern in the early 1980s was a new federal immigration law. The 1986 Immigration Reform and Control Act offered legal status, or amnesty, to those who could prove that they had lived continuously in the United States since before 1982. Many Mexican workers who were used to spending most of the year north of the border took advantage of this provision and became legal U.S. residents. At the same time, the new law set stiff new penalties for hiring undocumented workers—employers could now be fined from $250 to $10,000 per worker. By putting the burden on the employers, the authors of the law hoped to discourage them from hiring illegal aliens—and thus remove the lure that drew so many illegals into the United States.

Some employers of seasonal farmworkers were exempt

from the law, however, and in any case enforcement proved difficult. Once across the border, undocumented workers might travel anywhere in the United States to find jobs. Tracking them down was a tall order, and the Immigration and Naturalization Service (INS) was hard-pressed to do it. Thus the flow of illegal aliens slowed briefly when the new law took effect, and then resumed. Overall, the number of Mexicans in the United States jumped from fewer than 9 million to 12.6 million in the 1980s.

A QUESTION OF SOCIAL SERVICES

As Mexican migration surged, so did resentment of the immigrants, fueled in part by another economic downturn in the United States. By the 1990s, tension over immigration issues had reached a high point. "The climate is now as nasty as it has ever been, and getting nastier every day," a Washington, D.C., immigrant advocate commented in 1992.[5] The Mexican border was described as a "war zone," and human-rights groups accused border authorities of "appalling" abuses in their efforts to keep illegal immigrants out and to deport those who were already in the United States.

In contrast, conservatives such as Pat Buchanan, a candidate for the Republican presidential nomination in 1992 and 1996, urged even tighter border controls, warning that America's European heritage could be "diluted" by the flow. Others asserted that immigrants were abusing the extensive social welfare services of the United States. A Mexican woman, they said, could take advantage of U.S. medical services to have a baby; then, because her child was born in the United States and was therefore a U.S. citizen, she could stay in the country and receive welfare payments.

Whether there were actually enough such cases to cause

a strain on social services wasn't clear, but growing numbers of people became convinced that there were. Groups such as the Federation for American Immigration Reform began to campaign for stricter limits on immigration. In 1994, Californians passed Proposition 187, a ballot initiative that would deny undocumented aliens medical services and education. A court fight seemed likely to delay its effects, but some conservatives urged even stronger measures—denying social services to all immigrants, legal or not. (Not surprisingly, applications for citizenship soared as a result.) And when California Governor Pete Wilson, a strong supporter of Proposition 187, announced plans to seek the 1996 Republican presidential nomination, immigration seemed to be shaping up as a major campaign issue.

The debate was fueled by census figures showing that nearly 9 percent of the U.S. population was foreign-born—the highest percentage since World War II and twice what the percentage had been in 1970. Even moderates began to call for a new round of immigration reforms.

In 1995 a federal commission, formed five years earlier to advise Congress on immigration policy and made up of members of both parties, proposed reducing the total number of immigrants allowed into the country each year, charging employers a substantial fee for hiring skilled foreign workers, and taking steps to ensure that new immigrants would learn English and adopt American ways. Several bills that would limit immigration were introduced in Congress.

ENFORCEMENT

While Congress debated changes in the law, the Border Patrol stepped up enforcement, beginning major crackdowns at traditional entry points such as El Paso, Texas, and San

Ysidro, California. New fencing, new lights, and hundreds of new agents helped slow the flow at these points. But many of the would-be immigrants simply moved to less closely watched sections of the border, crossing into rural areas of Texas and Arizona. Others obtained forged identity documents to cross at the checkpoints. They had to wait longer to cross, and they had to pay more to the "coyotes," or guides, who helped them. But they were determined to cross.

Here is the story of one young man, twenty-one-year old Baltazar Trinidad Guadalupe, from a small town north of Mexico City. Late in 1995 Trinidad learned from relatives that there was work to be had laying sheetrock in Houston—work that might pay $12,000 a year, compared to the $1,500 he had earned doing odd jobs in Mexico that year. He tried several times to cross the border at Ciudad Juárez, but each time he was caught in the tightened security around El Paso. Then he heard that crossing might be easier at Matamoros, so he went there. A few minutes before midnight on a dark night in early February 1996, he waded across the Rio Grande into Brownsville, Texas, with a group of other Mexican workers—and was promptly caught by the Border Patrol. Returned to Mexico, Trinidad was still determined to enter the United States. "I will try it again," he told a reporter. "I have set a goal. Houston is my goal."[6]

THE CALL OF MONEY

The immigration problem just wouldn't go away, and that wasn't surprising. The great attraction north of the border was, and remains, money. The wages Mexican workers earn in California, Texas, and other U.S. job markets, while low by U.S. standards, are often six to ten times what they can expect to earn at home. Enough of that money is sent to the workers' families in Mexico to make it a significant factor in the Mexican economy. In some northern Mexican towns, for example, as much as a fourth of the people live part-time in the United States, channeling income back home. In the 1990s, a growing number of young men from Mexico City and other major urban centers in the heart of Mexico began to join the traditional flow of migrants from the rural north, giving U.S. wages an even wider impact.

In the past, this migration has served as a sort of pressure valve, helping to ease the impact of severe economic and social problems, so the Mexican government has never actively tried to halt it. Unlike the U.S. Border Patrol, which aims to stop illegal immigration, Mexico's special border police unit, Grupo Beta, is mainly concerned with culling criminals from the huge numbers of people who are constantly moving through the border towns and preventing them from preying on honest migrants. This attitude annoys American officials, who think Mexico should do more. Some Americans have even charged that Mexico at times encourages emigration, exporting its social problems to the north.

The reality is that stopping migration across the United States–Mexican border would be difficult even if both countries cracked down. As long as huge disparities in earning power remain, Mexican workers will most likely keep heading north. In the heat of the 1995 debate over immigration, Lucas Guttentag, an advocate of immigrant rights, noted:

> The United States, like every nation, has the right to control its borders. But a wise policy recognizes that real solutions can be achieved only by addressing the root causes of immigration and by attacking exploitation of immigrants. . . . People come to the United States not to receive social services but because global events cause them to be uprooted or because unscrupulous

employers want to exploit them. As long as the immigration debate is dominated by those who willfully ignore these realities, we will be forever distracted from addressing international migration issues in a meaningful and constructive way.[7]

In the end, the causes underlying Mexican immigration to the United States are economic ones, just as the problems created by immigration are linked to economic issues, such as trade and investment, between the two countries.

Mexico City is the financial center of Mexico. Here, students learn about the Mexican stock exchange from an observation deck.

5

• • •

DOLLARS AND PESOS

The 1992 U.S. presidential election offered no shortage of political rhetoric and "sound bites" designed to grab the attention of jaded voters. One of the most memorable of these was offered up by Texas businessman H. Ross Perot, who ran as an independent candidate. All along the Mexican border, Perot asserted, he could hear a "giant sucking sound" as U.S. manufacturing plants moved south, taking American jobs with them.

Specifically, Perot was warning against the effects of the North American Free Trade Agreement (NAFTA), a three-way pact designed to increase the flow of trade and investment between the United States, Mexico, and Canada. NAFTA was one of the hottest issues of the election campaign, and it remained controversial even after it was formally adopted the following year. But even before NAFTA,

Mexico and the United States were major trading partners, and many U.S. companies had already opened plants south of the border to take advantage of labor costs that were lower, and regulations that were looser than those at home. NAFTA was, in short, just the next phase in a relationship that had linked the Mexican and American economies ever since the days of Porfirio Díaz.

BUILDING INDUSTRY

After 1910, when the revolutionary leaders who followed Díaz closed the door to the massive foreign investment that the dictator had cultivated, Mexicans endured some hard years. Investors from the United States and other countries had frequently taken advantage of Mexico under Díaz, wielding so much influence that they exercised what amounted to a sort of economic imperialism. But they had also brought in cash and credit, helped build railroads that could move people and goods throughout the country, and developed the oil and mining industries. A switch to the sort of nationalist policy called for in the Mexican constitution of 1917, with the government taking a leading role in the economy, would have been difficult under the best circumstances and the most stable political climate. And in Mexico at that time, with civil war raging throughout the country, Mexican leaders rarely had a chance to map out such a policy in detail, much less put one into action.

As a result, the Mexican economy virtually collapsed, and then drifted for the better part of two decades. It only began to revive in the late 1930s when, under President Cárdenas, the government nationalized the oil industry, took over the railroads, and revived land reform. Even then, however, economic growth was still extremely slow. The United States and the other countries of the world were gripped by the Great Depression, and Mexico could not escape its effects. It remained at heart an agricultural country, relying on imports for most manufactured goods.

It took World War II to get the Mexican economy moving again. Mexico suddenly found that its oil and other raw materials were in great demand. At the same time, the war made imported goods scarce. Scores of new Mexican businesses were set up practically overnight to fill the demand for products that had once been imported. In this unchecked wartime boom, many manufacturers made fortunes charging high prices for goods that were often poor quality. But the wartime import shortage also woke up the country to the benefits of a self-sufficient manufacturing and industrial base. Even before the end of World War II, the government began to take steps to parlay the boom into an extended period of economic growth.

To develop new industries, the government stepped back a bit from the nationalist policies of the 1917 constitution. Private companies, Mexican leaders believed, could transform the country from a nation of rural peasants and farmers, or *campesinos*, to a modern industrial state—if the government created the right climate and offered incentives for them to do so. One of the government's most important tools in this process was a policy called Import Substitution Industrialization (ISI). Under this policy, so that new Mexican firms would not have to face competition from established manufacturers abroad, imported goods were kept out of the country with high barriers—at first, tariffs (taxes) that raised the cost of imported goods by as much as 100 percent; later, a system of import licenses that directly limited the supply.

At the same time, the government arranged for Mexican industries to get oil, electricity, rail transportation, and even bank credit at low rates, and it taxed their profits minimally—sometimes not at all. And, to encourage investors to put money into Mexican firms, the government relaxed its earlier rules on foreign investment. A law restricting foreign ownership to 49 percent of any Mexican firm stayed on the books, but it was overlooked to allow multinational companies to set up subsidiaries in Mexico. Although Mexican-owned industries (both private and state run) were at the center of the country's transformation, these foreign-owned companies played a key role.

American firms were among the first across the border. Not only was there a long tradition of U.S. investment in Mexico, but the industrial nations of Europe were reeling from the effects of World War II and needed to rebuild their own industries before they could venture abroad. That created an opening. In the years after the war, U.S. carmakers set up subsidiaries to build cars in Mexico; U.S. tire makers built plants there, too. Food processing, pharmaceuticals and cosmetics, and electric appliances were other areas that drew American companies. Soon Mexican consumers were driving cars, watching televisions, eating breakfast cereals, and drinking soft drinks made in Mexico by U.S. firms.

Beginning in 1965, the Mexican government also allowed U.S. companies to set up factories—*maquiladoras*—along the border where imported components could be assembled and the finished products shipped back to the United States with little or no export duty or tariff.

While the government nurtured manufacturing industries, it also began to shift away from the revolutionary call for land reform. In fact, with a few brief exceptions, Mexican leaders had always been far readier to pay lip service to land reform than to do much about it. Now, especially in the northwest, the government started irrigation projects to encourage "agribusiness"—big, privately owned farms that used the latest farming technology to grow cash crops such as cotton and winter vegetables. Much of the produce was meant for export to the United States. Tourism also became a big part of postwar economy, and the government invested heavily in the development of resorts such as Acapulco.

All this helped fuel a remarkable period of growth. For more than thirty years, from World War II into the 1970s, Mexico enjoyed an average annual economic growth rate of 6 percent. It was held up to the world as a model for developing nations.[1] But there were flaws in the model. Manufacturers grew used to government subsidies and tax breaks; and safe behind the protective legal wall that kept out foreign competition, they were free to turn out shoddy goods at high prices. To keep this happy (in their eyes) situation in place, they sought political influence, sometimes openly but often with bribes and other under-the-table methods.

On the government side, a huge bureaucracy grew up, devoted to the care and feeding of industry. It was sometimes hard to tell where government left off and industry began. The government owned many industries outright and was heavily involved in real-estate development and scores of other ventures (a practice that allowed many officials to grow rich by doing deals on the side), and leaders in private industry enjoyed extraordinary access to government. The chairman of one of the largest Mexican conglomerates, Alfa Group, had a direct line to the president.

Meanwhile, Mexico's move to an industrial economy ignored the needs of the poor, especially the rural poor. Delaying land reform actually helped industries grow, since plenty of landless peasants were available to join the workforce at new factories. But one result of this was a tremendous movement of people from the country to the cities, in particular Mexico City. Mexico City's population grew from 3.4 million in 1950 to 15 million in 1980, and it was expected to top 25 million before the year 2000. That made Mexico City the world's second-largest city, after Tokyo, Japan. The old city center was ringed by new apartment buildings and, increasingly, by slums.

A high birthrate added to the country's problems. The country's population grew from less than 20 million before World War II to more than 50 million in 1970, and it was expected to top 120 million by the year 2000. Even with booming economic growth, there simply weren't enough jobs. Unemployment became a serious problem. The government was pledged to provide education and health care and other services for the people. It also subsidized transportation and basic foods—to the tune of $1 billion a year for corn, beans, and cooking oil—and it struggled to create jobs for the unemployed. These demands couldn't be ignored; that would be risking political unrest and even revolution. But, coupled with the continued need to subsidize industrial development, the costs of meeting them outstripped the government's resources. Mexico began to borrow, and borrow heavily, abroad.

THE PROMISE OF OIL

For a while, in the late 1970s, oil wealth seemed to promise a way out of the dilemma. Through the 1970s, a series of new finds revealed that Mexico had more than ten times as much oil as had been previously thought; in fact, it had the fifth-largest oil reserves and seventh-largest natural-gas reserves in the world. At the same time, because of attempts by the Organization of Petroleum Exporting Countries (OPEC) to control the world oil market, and because of other international factors, the price of oil took a series of enormous leaps. The government poured money into the development of new oil fields and wells, through the state-run oil company Pemex. Oil production soared, and so did oil exports.

In the five years from 1976 to 1981, Mexico's exports quintupled, and oil accounted for most of that increase, rising from 10 percent of total exports to nearly 75 percent.[2]

No country was happier for Mexico's good fortune than the United States. A boycott by oil-producing Arab states in 1973, and OPEC's attempts to control the oil supply since then, had shown the United States the dangers of dependence on imported oil. Many Americans were also becoming aware that the world's oil supply wasn't endless—sooner or later, it would run out. Facing an "energy crisis," the United States began to take steps to use less imported oil, increase its own production, and develop alternate energy sources. These new programs would take time to put into place, however. Americans were delighted to find that there were huge oil reserves right next door.

Mexico did not join OPEC because it did not want to be bound by the cartel's production caps and because it wanted to be free to sell its oil wherever, and at whatever price, it wished. But so much of the country's oil and natural gas exports flowed to the United States in the late 1970s that in 1980 the government, fearful of becoming too dependent on the U.S. market, adopted a new policy: No more than half of crude-oil exports would go to any one client. Energy issues also led to new disputes between the countries, overpricing, and environmental damage. Oil spills, for example, didn't respect international boundaries, and oil that escaped from wells along Mexico's gulf coast ended up on beaches in Texas. Mexico spent $50 million to cap one well, Ixtoc I, that went out of control in 1979 and poured oil into the gulf at a rate of 30,000 barrels a day.

Such costs were only a small part of the huge expenses involved in increasing oil production, which were added to the financial burdens the government already carried. The costs exceeded oil revenues; but as the extent of the bonanza became known, Mexico had no trouble borrowing money from banks in the United States and other countries. By the early 1980s, Mexico had the largest foreign debt in the developing world, approaching $80 billion. A handful of big U.S. banks had lent more than $16 billion, an amount that equaled 40 percent of their reserves.

However, oil didn't turn out to be the economic cure-all that Mexico and its creditors hoped. The country's feverish growth fueled inflation, so that by 1981 the costs of goods and services were increasing at a rate of 30 percent a year—and the rate was rising. The poor were more hard-pressed than ever; the rich began to convert their holdings in Mexican currency (pesos) to U.S. dollars, so their wealth would retain its value. Then came a sharp drop in world oil prices, reducing Mexico's income, and a sharp rise in the interest rates charged by international lenders. By 1982 Mexico didn't have enough money to make payments on its loans, and it was plunged into a financial crisis.

An international rescue package saved the day. If Mexico were to default on its loans, some of the largest U.S. banks would be threatened with collapse—with disastrous effects on the U.S. and world economies. To head off that threat, the United States put up some $2 billion in advance payments and guarantees for oil and food imports from Mexico. Nearly $4 billion in new loans were negotiated through the International Monetary Fund (IMF), in exchange for Mexico's promise to begin an austerity program and put its finances in order following IMF guidelines. And private banks agreed to give Mexico an extension on its loan payments.

Mexico emerged from the crisis, but the effects were severe. The peso had fallen in value from roughly twenty-five to the dollar in 1981 to more than one hundred to the dollar in the fall of 1982, shrinking the value of average people's savings and their purchasing power. Inflation hit 100 percent at the worst of the crisis, and growth was stopped cold.[3]

Much of the burden of digging out of the pile of debt the country had amassed fell on average and poor people. Already battered by inflation, they were hit again when the government, trying to put a stop to the snowballing debt and follow the IMF guidelines, sharply raised prices for the goods and services it provided. For most Mexicans, times were as hard as they had been during the 1930s. It was as if the "miracle" of industrial growth had never occurred.

OPENING TRADE

When Miguel de la Madrid Hurtado took office as president of Mexico on December 1, 1982, he realized that the country needed a radical change in economic policy. That view was shared by his planning and budget secretary, Carlos Salinas de Gortari, who would follow him in office. Both leaders saw that the policies that had protected and subsidized Mexican industries since World War II were now a drag on the economy. Around the world, countries were dropping barriers to trade, turning state-run industry over to private hands, and competing in a global marketplace. But Mexico, by protecting its own industries from the competition of imports, had all but guaranteed that its products wouldn't be competitive abroad—they cost too much and were too poorly made. Now, if the country wanted to continue to grow, it would have to play by world rules.

Under de la Madrid, Mexico joined the General Agreement on Tariffs and Trade (GATT), an international organization made up of more than one hundred countries pledged to reducing tariffs and other barriers to trade. The government also negotiated new trade agreements with the United States. The protectionist walls tumbled down—within just a few years of joining GATT, Mexico dropped licensing requirements for 95 percent of the goods it imported, and it reduced its highest tariffs from 100 percent to 20 percent. The government also reorganized Pemex, the state-run oil company, and sold off hundreds of state-owned industries, including the national telephone company and airline. By the mid-1980s, the number of state-owned companies had shrunk from more than 1,000 to just over 200.[4] Government bureaucracy and spending shrank as well. Under Salinas, who took office in 1988, the government actually ran a budget surplus.

These policies helped trigger a new boom in Mexico, and this time American firms played an even larger part. U.S. exports to Mexico rose until, for the first time in many years, their value exceeded the value of goods (mainly oil) imported from Mexico. And all kinds of United States-owned businesses opened south of the border. The most visible were big retail chains—Kmart and Wal-Mart opened stores in Mexico, and by 1993 there were scores of 7-Eleven stores and McDonald's restaurants.[5] Along the border, a growing number of companies took advantage of easier regulations and set up *maquiladoras*.

By turning away from protectionism, Mexico laid the groundwork for NAFTA, an agreement it never could have signed under its previous policies. The pact was designed to eliminate most tariffs and other trade barriers between Canada, Mexico, and the United States over a fifteen-year period beginning January 1, 1994. It cemented changes that had already taken place, expanded the scope of others, and required significant changes in Mexico's laws about investment, financial services, and other economic matters.

NAFTA required legislative approval in all three countries, and it sparked sharp debate. Mexican opponents of the agreement charged that it favored the United States and Canada and would return the country to the days of Díaz, allowing United States interests to run the economy. Porfirio Muñoz Ledo, a Mexican senator of the opposition Democratic Revolution Party (PRD), called it a "colonial" agreement that would "turn our country over to the foreigners."[6] However, the majority Institutional Revolutionary Party (PRI), which had negotiated the pact, held sixty-one of the senate's sixty-four seats, so approval was never in doubt. Canadians also approved the treaty, after some initial concerns over provisions covering energy, grain, and other specific areas.

In the United States, the debate was fierce and wide-ranging. Although NAFTA had been negotiated under a Republican president, George Bush, it was endorsed by Democratic President Bill Clinton when he took office in 1993, as well as by many business and financial leaders. Support for the treaty was strongest in the South and West, which stood to benefit most from increased trade with Mexico.

But opposition was also strong. Northern and eastern states, which had been losing jobs for years as manufacturers moved plants south or overseas, feared that NAFTA would set off a new round of plant closings and layoffs by businesses attracted to Mexico's low labor costs. Organized labor agreed and opposed the treaty vehemently. The Democratic Party was split, some supporting Clinton and some taking labor's side. "It's not fair to ask American workers to compete against Mexican workers who earn $1 an hour," Congressman David Bonior, a Democrat from Michigan, told the House of Representatives in an impassioned speech against the pact.[7]

The treaty's most outspoken critic was H. Ross Perot, the

Texas billionaire who had failed in his 1992 bid to capture the presidency as an independent. Perot attacked NAFTA in a book and held a series of rallies to muster opposition to it. In November 1993, with the congressional vote on the treaty fast approaching, the pros and cons were laid out in a sharp, often bitter televised debate between Perot and Vice President Al Gore. United States companies, Perot argued, would move production south of the border to take advantage not only of low wages but also of weak labor unions and loose environmental regulations. (The uncomplimentary picture he painted of Mexico prompted much anger there.) Gore countered that the treaty would actually create jobs in the United States because exports to Mexico and Canada would increase, fueling economic growth. He also argued that NAFTA would give the United States leverage in getting Mexico to raise wages and improve environmental standards. Public opinion shifted in favor of the treaty after the debate, and it won narrow approval in Congress.

The initial effects of NAFTA included a jump in trade—U.S. exports to Mexico increased by nearly $16 billion in 1994.[8] Large American firms expanded their operations, and, under streamlined permit procedures, a growing number of Americans set up small businesses in Mexico. However, NAFTA's critics warned that the benefits were illusory—America was exporting machine tools, materials, and components for manufacturing and assembly plants, while importing finished goods from Mexico.

Mexico, meanwhile, still faced serious problems. With trade barriers down, Mexican businesses had to make major changes to compete with foreign firms at home and to win a place for their products in world markets. Those that could not change quickly enough faced bankruptcy. The country's long-neglected *campesinos* were threatened by imports of grain from the United States and Canada; they couldn't hope to compete with the huge mechanized farms of the Great Plains. New factories might provide jobs for some who could no longer make a living by farming, but not for all. Like past booms, Mexico's latest spurt of economic growth promised to make paupers as well as millionaires—and that was a matter of concern to the United States.

THE PESO CRISIS

With NAFTA binding the United States and Mexico in an ever-tighter relationship, Mexico's problems were increasingly problems for the United States. The importance of their relationship was underscored in early 1995, when the Mexican economy plunged into one of its worst crises in modern times. Once again, mounting foreign debt ($160 billion) and rising interest rates helped create it. Privately, American officials had warned the Mexican government in 1994 that the debt was rising out of control. But 1994 was an election year, and the government was unwilling to make the cutbacks that would be necessary if its borrowing was curtailed.

The crisis was triggered in December 1994, after Ernesto Zedillo Ponce de León took office as Mexico's new president. An economist, Zedillo looked at the country's huge debt and decided that the only logical course was a devaluation of the peso. This unexpected step threw financial markets into turmoil. Some $29 billion of Mexico's debt consisted of short-term bonds payable in pesos or dollars. As the peso lost value, investors demanded to be paid in dollars. Mexico didn't have the reserves to do that, and investors suddenly faced huge losses. Many panicked and began to pull money out of Mexican investments and investments in other developing countries. Once again, Mexico's financial turmoil threatened United States and international finance.

The United States cobbled together a $50 billion rescue

package that included $30 billion in new loans from the IMF and the central banks of industrial countries, with the U.S. Treasury providing $20 billion in loans and guarantees that Mexico would meet its obligations. Mexico agreed to a new package of reforms and restrictions, and it promised to raise more than $12 billion by selling off more state-run enterprises, including railways, electrical power plants, and numerous other operations.

The bailout helped ease the crisis, but it had plenty of critics, who charged that U.S. taxpayers were being forced to cover the losses of investors who had simply gambled unwisely. Congressional leaders demanded that the United States attach strings to the plan—provisions that would require Mexico to buy more American products, raise wages closer to the American scale, or put up shares in Pemex as collateral against new loans.

The Clinton administration defended the plan. Not only did the crisis threaten international banking, administration officials said, but the United States needed Mexico as an export market. One immediate effect of the peso's drop in value was to make Mexican imports cheap in the United States and American goods too costly for most Mexicans to afford. A strong peso and a strong Mexican economy would help keep U.S. exports flowing across the border, so the bailout plan served broad American economic interests. Moreover, if the United States tried to force the Mexican government to agree to stringent conditions like those proposed in Congress, Mexicans would see that, once again, the United States was exercising a sort of economic imperialism over its southern neighbor. If the Mexican government agreed, it would lose popular support and, possibly, collapse.

The peso crisis raised other risks, the administration warned. A flood of migrants would head north if the Mexican economy collapsed, increasing illegal immigration along the United States–Mexican border by as much as 30 percent. And the more Mexico struggled to restore stability to its economy, the less it was able to deal with crucial issues that were the legacy of industrial development, including poverty and pollution. It faced new threats of political unrest and a rise in criminal activity, including drug trafficking. These problems, too, the United States could not ignore.

The smuggling of drugs and currency between Mexico and the United States is a growing concern. U.S. Customs agents frequently use dogs to check for hidden drugs.

6

NEW TIMES, NEW ISSUES

More scenes from the border: Children escape the heat by splashing in the clouded water of a canal that drains an industrial park. When the wind is right, acrid, noxious fumes drift through the air, making people cough and rub their stinging eyes. Wastes go from houses into slow-moving open sewers, which are lined with thick, black sludge.

Mexico and the United States have been dealing with issues of territory, immigration, and trade from the beginning. But new times have brought new concerns to complicate the relationship between the two countries. Among the most urgent of these are environmental problems, like those described above, mostly caused by industrial pollution. A second area of concern is drug trafficking—the flow of illegal drugs from Mexico into the United States, once a trickle, has increased sharply. Dealing with both these concerns will require new levels of cooperation between the countries.

A SHARED ENVIRONMENT

Pollution is a problem in virtually every industrialized country. But Mexico's rush to industrialization and the rapid growth of its cities has produced serious environmental problems throughout the country. Mexico City, its air fouled by fumes from automobiles and gas used for cooking in millions of homes, has one of the world's worst air-pollution problems. The problems that bear most directly on United States–Mexican relations, however, are those along the border, where by the early 1990s the unchecked growth of *maquiladoras* had produced some real environmental nightmares.

Many of the border factories were assembly plants that produced relatively harmless products. But some produced toxic chemicals, and regulations governing their operations were not as strict (or not as strictly enforced) as regulations in the United States. Chemical wastes from industrial processes found their way into the air and into the water of the Rio Grande and other streams and rivers in the border region. Smoke from power plants, burning high-sulfur oil to produce electricity for the factories, clouded the air, drifting north or south of the border as the wind changed.

Factories and power plants were not the only sources of the problem. Pesticide runoff from farms (on both sides of the border) added to river pollution. Far upstream from the border, mining operations dumped toxic chemicals into the Rio Grande. And as people flocked to the border region to take jobs in the factories, the population of towns and cities grew so quickly that city services, such as sewage and water lines, couldn't keep up. For example, the once-sleepy Mexican town of Matamoros, on the Rio Grande, grew to a city of 600,000 without sewage treatment facilities. Raw sewage flowed into open canals in the *colonias*, the crowded clusters of makeshift housing where many workers lived, and from there into the river. Residents carried water in buckets from distant community taps to their tiny, ramshackle homes. In 1991 plans were finally made to build two sewage treatment plants and to run water and sewer lines to the *colonias*. But many of the factory workers could not afford to pay their share of the cost of installing the service, estimated at $380, because they earned just $50 to $90 a week.[1]

The situation was the same in many other towns along the border. The *maquiladoras* were built in Mexico, but the pollution affected people on both sides, and not only by creating an acrid stench in the air and making water unfit for drinking or swimming. Increased cases of asthma, bronchitis, skin rashes, and other illnesses were reported. There were alarming increases in the rates of cancer and birth defects. Brownsville, Texas—a mere fifty feet from Matamoros, just across the Rio Grande—reported a 230 percent increase in cancer among school-age children between 1991 and 1993.[2]

Both countries have taken steps to solve at least some of the environmental problems, working individually and together. A joint commission, the International Boundary and Water Commission (IBWC), has addressed pollution of rivers and streams along the border. Made up of United States and Mexican sections, the IBWC was formed in 1944 to handle flood control, water conservation, and other issues related to the use of waters that both countries share. In the 1990s, pollution has become one of its main concerns. The commission has been involved in constructing several sewage treatment plants, as well as conducting studies of the levels of toxic pollution in the Rio Grande and in the groundwaters of the border region.

The IBWC's efforts address only part of the problem, however, and concerns about the environment were on center stage during the debate over the North American Free Trade Agreement (NAFTA) in 1993. Critics of the agreement warned that, by encouraging United States firms to do business in Mexico's less strictly regulated climate, the trade pact would lead to more pollution. As a result, Canada, Mexico, and the United States signed an environmental side agreement to the treaty. It created another international group, the Commission for Environmental Cooperation, to handle problems that affected them jointly.

In 1995 the commission got its first case, brought jointly by Mexican environmental groups and the National Audubon Society of the United States. It was one of the worst bird kills in North American history: Some 40,000 migratory birds, of species that annually winter in Mexico and summer in the United States and Canada, died at a polluted reservoir in central Mexico. Wastes from nearby tanneries and a chemical plant were suspected, but an investigation by Mexican authorities failed to pin down the cause of the kill. The commission was to find out the cause, locate the source of the pollution, and recommend steps to correct the problem. Its work was certain to be closely watched because, if the group was successful, it could serve as a model for international cooperation on environmental problems.

The Mexican government, for its part, has staunchly defended its record in environmental protection. And, while Mexico clearly lagged behind the United States and Canada in this area, it was taking steps to solve its serious pollution problems. It passed stiffer environmental laws and hired more inspectors to enforce them. But, especially after the financial crisis hit in 1995, there was not enough money to find and fix all the problems. Moreover, close ties between industry and government often meant that major industrial polluters were not called to account and made to stop their actions.

THE PATRONES

As trade and immigration increased along the United States-Mexican border in the 1980s and 1990s, so did shipments of illegal drugs. By 1995, Mexico had become a major supplier of illegal drugs to the United States, funneling cocaine and white heroin from Colombia, white heroin and hashish from Asia, and homegrown marijuana and "black tar" heroin into the country through a network to cities such as Los Angeles, Seattle, Chicago, Dallas, Houston, and New York.

Marijuana and small amounts of other drugs had passed across the Mexican border at least since the 1960s. The problem had flared up in 1969, when the United States launched Operation Intercept. For days, all vehicles headed into the United States were stopped and checked for drugs. Besides tying up traffic along the border, the action infuriated the Mexican government, which hadn't been warned or consulted. It didn't stop drug traffic, which continued to grow. In the 1980s, Mexico increasingly became a way station for drugs being smuggled into the United States from other countries.

The new drug traffic was thought to be largely controlled by a half dozen *patrones*, or bosses, based in cities along the border—Tijuana, Ciudad Juárez, and Matamoros—as well as cities farther south. They included men such as Amado Carillo Fuentes, considered to be Mexico's most powerful drug lord; Juan García Ábrego, on the FBI's most-wanted list, with a $2 million reward for his capture; and Joaquin Guzman (nicknamed Chapo, or Shorty), who, before his arrest in 1993, dug tunnels under the border to take drugs into Arizona and California. Many Mexican drug traffickers began as shippers for Colombian cartels. As their contacts and expertise grew, they set up operations of their own, bringing huge shipments of cocaine into Mexico aboard converted commercial passenger jets and container ships. As they grew in power and wealth, the *patrones* began to buy into legitimate businesses that could help them in the drug trade, such as trucking companies to transport the drugs and banks through which they could launder their profits.

The drug trade flourished despite efforts on both sides of the border to end it. Tons of marijuana, cocaine, and other drugs were seized entering Mexico, passing through, and at the U.S. border, but with thousands of trucks and cars crossing the international boundary legally each day, and so many miles of border unpatrolled, stopping all drug shipments was impossible. American law enforcement officials laid much of the blame for the continuing traffic on their Mexican counterparts. A former agent for the U.S. Drug Enforcement Agency (DEA) told a reporter: "They could hit the traffickers any time they wanted to. But who is going to knock off the goose that lays the golden eggs?" Mexico, the agency estimated, was earning $7 billion a year from illegal drugs.[3]

THE CORRUPTION QUESTION

Drug traffickers were able to operate brazenly, it was charged, because in many cases they were protected by government officials and even by the police. Bribes and payoffs were common at local and regional levels. The *New York Times* chronicled these abuses. One of the most wanted traffickers of the 1980s, Manuel Salcido (known as El Cochiloco, or the Mad Pig), lived in luxury for years on his ranch in Colima, often entertaining the governor. After Felix Gallardo, called the "godfather" of the Mexican drug trade, was arrested in 1989, he was allowed to continue his operations from a suite in a Mexico City jail, set up with cellular phones and a fax machine. In 1991, soldiers shot and killed seven federal drug agents who chased traffickers to a secret landing strip in Veracruz State; the soldiers apparently had been protecting a drug shipment. In June 1995, the government had to use army troops to capture Hector Luis Palma in Guadalajara; the city's federal police detachment was so corrupt that the entire force was arrested along with him. Even high-ranking officials were accused of closing their eyes to the illegal drug trade in exchange for money. One of those so accused was Javier Coello Trejo, who headed Mexico's drug-enforcement efforts from late 1988 to 1990. Guillermo Gonzalez Calderoni, a former chief of federal police drug enforcement, was ordered arrested on corruption charges in 1993.[4] Other officials were dismissed on suspicion of corruption, although none was prosecuted.

Corruption was not universal. Mexican law enforcement officials made scores of arrests and countless seizures of illegal drugs, and sometimes they paid a high price for taking action. Drug traffickers were linked to the murders of a police chief in Tijuana and a number of state prosecutors and federal police officers who tried to enforce drug laws. Mexican officials strongly defended their efforts, pointing out that drug trafficking would disappear without the demand for illegal drugs and the distribution networks north of the border. Still, corruption was widespread enough that U.S. drug enforcement officials were increasingly reluctant to share information or work with their Mexican counterparts.

Apart from the fact that traffickers had managed to gain at least some influence at nearly all levels of government, Mexican officials had reasons not to dig too deeply into the underground world of drugs. The government was not in a position to pour resources into an all-out fight with the traffickers—a fight that could bring new levels of violence, terrorism, and assassination to Mexico. And drugs were fast becoming an important sector of the economy, producing income on which growing numbers of people depended.

Traffickers and corrupt officials were not the only ones to profit. Poor farmers, especially rural Indians, the most isolated and poverty-stricken group in Mexican society, were enticed by drug dealers to plant marijuana and opium poppies among the corn plants in their fields. These crops could bring in more in a single season than the Indians could otherwise expect to earn in several years. But drug dealers often used threats and force, instead of money, to get the produce. Indian leaders who objected were shot. In some remote parts of the Sierra Madre, drug-related violence all but wiped out small settlements. Federal agents searched the countryside by helicopter, looking for drug crops (but, it was said, not looking too hard).

Through the 1980s and into the 1990s, the growing importance of drug production and trafficking, and their influence on Mexico's society and government, were watched with concern in the United States. Mexico seemed set to become another Colombia, where the drug industry was so entrenched that eliminating it seemed impossible. U.S. leaders repeatedly pressured Mexico to do more against drug trafficking, and U.S. law enforcement agencies launched actions against border drug traffic. But American officials also tacitly recognized the dilemmas Mexico faced and were often willing to let their concern about drugs take a backseat while they dealt with other priorities.

In the early 1990s, top priority went to the negotiation and approval of NAFTA. Knowing that the treaty's chances of approval would be hurt if Mexico was seen as a corrupt, drug-ridden country, they downplayed drugs. "People desperately wanted drugs not to become a complicating factor for NAFTA. There was a degree of illicit activity that was just accepted," a former drug enforcement official for the Bush administration said.[5] Instead, the United States focused its efforts on Colombia, Bolivia, and other countries that were the source of many of the drugs that passed through Mexico. Meanwhile, Mexico's drug lords became more firmly established, strengthening their bases in Mexico and expanding their networks in the United States.

When Ernesto Zedillo was inaugurated as president late in 1994, American officials expressed hope that the new administration would do a better job of cleaning up corruption and stamping out the drug trade. To underscore that point, the United States sent the new president a list of fifteen officials who were suspected of corruption, with the hope that they would not be appointed to positions in his government. They weren't, and after the United States helped put together the $50 billion rescue package in 1995, Mexico agreed to other steps—more open exchange of information about drug traffic, firmer steps to counter the laundering of drug profits, new actions against the traffickers themselves. Signaling the tougher approach, Mexican authorities arrested accused drug trafficker Juan García Ábrego and turned him over to United States law enforcement officials in January 1996.

Still, many Americans were not optimistic that Mexico's new broom would sweep clean. United States ambassador to Mexico James R. Jones warned: "If we don't do something, both in the southern United States and in Mexico, Mexico will take over from Colombia in a few years as the traffickers' headquarters of choice. It will undermine democracy. It will undermine commercial development. It will undermine free trade."[6]

*Mexico's flag, shown here with
the National Palace in the background,
was adopted in 1821.*

7

MEXICO AND DEMOCRACY

"I blame the government for all that is happening. The officials kept telling us that we were a first-world country, that we had become just like the United States. But that's not so, and all this proves it."[1]

The Mexico City cab driver who spoke those words in March 1995 expressed thoughts shared by many Mexicans. The situation he referred to was the recent peso crisis and a package of tough measures imposed by the government as a sort of economic shock treatment in its wake. To stop inflation and raise revenues, the government sharply raised taxes and prices for gasoline, electricity, transportation, and other basic items. Interest rates for mortgages and consumer loans soared as high as 100 percent.

The changes hit average Mexicans hard, in ways that rippled through the economy. People had less money to spend, so they bought less. Thousands of businesses, faced with higher costs and lower sales, went bankrupt, and workers lost their jobs. By midyear, the peso had regained some of its lost value, and prices on the Mexican stock market were climbing. Inflation had been reined in, and Mexican exports were up. But two million people were out of work—twice the number that were unemployed at the start of the year. The gap between rich and poor, already huge, grew larger. And increasingly, Mexicans were angry. "We need a capable government, not one that is always trying to hurt us," a Mexico City locksmith told a reporter for the *New York Times*. "They raise the price of electricity, of gas, of transportation, and then everything goes up. This country is rich, but it is governed by bad people."[2]

The anger and dissatisfaction spreading through Mexico's ninety-four million people increased the prospect of political unrest. The Institutional Revolutionary Party (PRI), which had controlled the government since the 1920s, had held onto power in 1994 elections. But the country had been rocked by a series of political assassinations, and the government was battling a peasant rebellion in the southern state of Chiapas. And to many observers, in Mexico and abroad, the country's economic and social problems seemed firmly linked to its politics.

RESENTMENT AND REBELLION

On January 1, 1994—the same day that NAFTA took effect—the Mexican government found itself faced with armed rebellion. In the southern state of Chiapas, the Zapatista National Liberation Army, made up mainly of Maya Indians, took over four towns and declared war on the government. A corrupt political system, the rebels charged, had exploited the Indians and driven them into poverty, while promoting the interests of rich ranchers and landlords. NAFTA was yet another blow, since impoverished *campesinos* had no hope of competing with agricultural imports from the huge farms of the north.

The government sent troops and quickly routed the rebels from the towns, in actions that cost more than 150 lives. The rebels' top leader, a mysterious masked man who went by the name Commandante Marcus, escaped, melting away into the jungle with his top aides. Rather than pursuing a military campaign against the Zapatistas, however, the government offered to talk. The fighting died down, and government officials sat down with masked rebel representatives to work out a settlement.

The rebels demanded an end to discrimination against Indians and to the widespread deprivation in Chiapas, and nationwide political reform. The government acknowledged that the rebels had some legitimate grievances; Chiapas, on the Guatemalan border, has long been one of the country's most remote and impoverished regions. The government offered more support for farmers; new roads, schools, industries, and job retraining programs; land reform; and new laws to protect Indian rights. It agreed to national reforms.

The Zapatistas rejected the proposals. In February 1996, the two sides finally agreed on a broadly worded pact designed to protect the rights of all of Mexico's ten million Indians. Talks on other issues, including land reform, continued.

The Zapatista rebellion seemed to pose no immediate threat to the government. But many of the problems that led to it permeated Mexican society: a widening gap between rich and poor, corruption that reached from the level of traffic police to top government officials, and a political system that had kept one party in power for seventy years. There was danger that if these problems were not addressed, political unrest would spread from Chiapas throughout the country.

Hundreds of local citizens' groups were already putting pressure on the government. Many of these groups had formed in the wake of a devastating earthquake that struck Mexico City in 1985, killing as many as 10,000 people and destroying four hundred buildings. The government had been slow to respond to the enormous needs—for housing, health care, and other services—created by the quake, so people had organized to demand action. Gradually these groups had broadened their concerns to include the corruption and election fraud that had helped keep the PRI in power.

ONE-PARTY POLITICS

The PRI was founded in 1928, in the wake of the 1910 revolution and the civil turmoil that followed it. From the beginning, the party had not tolerated serious challenges. Although Mexican presidents were chosen in elections that were supposedly free, and were limited to single six-year terms, the PRI held a monopoly on power. The party's candidates were handpicked by its leaders, and their victory was assured—by force and fraud if necessary. For sixty years, the party did not lose a presidential, gubernatorial, or senatorial election. Its firm hold on power gave opposition groups virtually no voice in politics and provided a fertile breeding ground for corruption.

Signs that the PRI's iron grip might be slipping began to appear in the late 1980s. In 1988, several hundred local citizens' groups joined forces to create the Civic Alliance, an umbrella organization that set up a national network of observers to monitor the presidential election in that year. Their work did change the outcome of the vote. When early returns showed Cuauhtémoc Cárdenas, the candidate of the leftist opposition Democratic Revolutionary Party (PRD), making a strong showing, the government finished the count in secret. Carlos Salinas de Gortari, the PRI candidate, was named the winner eight days later, and Cárdenas's ballots later turned up in dumpsters.[3] One result of that election was a split in the left, with some PRD members calling for radical antigovernment action. A second result was a movement toward genuine election reform, produced in part by pressure from the United States.

Mexico's political problems caused concern north of the border. The prospect of unrest, even revolt, made investors leery, and it made Mexico less attractive as a trading partner. American concern grew after NAFTA increased the U.S. stake in Mexico; by mid-1994, with a new Mexican presidential election looming, U.S. investments accounted for nearly two-thirds of all foreign investment in Mexico. Some members of Congress threatened to renegotiate the trade treaty if fraud marred the election. Even without that threat, the idea that American investors might pull out if political turmoil erupted was a third force pressuring the government for reform. One PRI official summed it up bluntly: "We have to have clean elections or we won't get the capital we need."[4]

As a result of all these pressures, the PRI and the Mexican government agreed to a series of measures designed to reduce, if not eliminate, election fraud. New voter registration procedures, limits on campaign financing and spending, and the appointment of independent citizens to the federal elections board were among changes enacted between 1990 and the August 1994 presidential vote.

Opposition parties were voted into power in three states and hundreds of towns during those years. But after sixty-six years of single-party politics, Mexicans had little faith that the reforms would change the federal government. Nearly half, polls showed, expected the 1994 presidential election to be corrupt.[5] And the campaign leading up to that vote was tumultuous. The PRI's first candidate, Luis Donaldo Colosio, was assassinated at a rally in Tijuana in March. A single deranged gunman was blamed—despite evidence that the candidate was shot from two directions. Many Mexicans suspected a conspiracy involving drug traffickers and politicians.

Ernesto Zedillo, who had been Colosio's campaign manager, took his place as the PRI's candidate and won the vote. The conservative National Action Party (PAN) finished second; the PRD, wracked by divisions, a distant third. The Civic Alliance and other groups presented evidence of fraud, including photocopied voter registration forms, but the fraud did not appear to be as blatant or as widespread as it had been in 1988. After Zedillo took office in December, he began fresh investigations into the killing of Colosio and of Jose Francisco Ruiz Massieu, a reform-minded PRI official who was shot in September 1994. (The Ruiz Massieu investigation led to the arrest of former president Salinas's brother Raul Salinas, who was accused of having ordered and paid for the killing.) The Zedillo government also agreed to negotiate with the main opposition parties on a series of political reforms that would lead to full democracy.

For the government, a driving force behind these moves was the peso crisis and the need to reassure foreign, especially U.S. investors about Mexico's stability. But whether the latest round of reforms would bring real change remained to be seen. "The government now finds itself forced by the economic crisis to reach a substantive political agreement," one opposition leader said. "What we don't know is how it will feel in a few months."[6]

BUILDING RESPECT

Geography and history made Mexico and the United States neighbors, beginning a relationship that neither country can escape or ignore. In the past, that relationship has included as much conflict as cooperation, and it has seldom been equal. First military power, and then economic clout, gave the United States the stronger hand. Today, Mexicans and Americans still view each other through the lens of their shared history—but the world is changing, and their relationship is changing with it.

Around the world, barriers to trade and investment are falling. Business and financial markets operate globally. Satellite communications make it possible to follow events and do business all over the world. Goods and people travel between countries with speed and freedom that would have been unthinkable a hundred years ago. In this changing world, both Mexico and the United States have recognized that free trade and the exports it generates are the best hope for new jobs and prosperity. That, at least, was the guiding principle behind NAFTA, which bound the two countries in their closest trade relationship ever.

But exports must have a market, and people who are desperately poor or caught up in political turmoil can't buy goods from abroad. As world trade increases, then, nations become more dependent on each other, and events that happen in one part of the world can have profound effects far away. The recognition that economic interdependence works two ways—down as well as up—was behind the actions that the United States took in 1995 to stabilize the teetering Mexican economy. President Bill Clinton warned then: "If we fail to act, the crisis of confidence in Mexico's economy could spread to other emerging countries in Latin America and Asia, the kind of markets that buy our goods and services today and that will buy far more of them in the future."[7]

Shoring up the Mexican economy was not simply a matter of economics, however. For the United States, it was also a matter of national security. A country's economic health is inseparable from its political stability—poverty and hardship breed unrest. In Mexico's case, as we have seen, poverty also contributes to a set of serious problems that affect the United States directly: drug trafficking, environmental pollution, illegal migration. American concerns over these problems led some people to call for a sort of financial arm-twisting, in exchange for help with its financial crisis, they said, Mexico should be required to police its border, to keep potential migrants away, and should allow U.S. drug enforcement agents to carry out operations in Mexican territory.

Mexicans viewed these demands as insults; one Mexico City newspaper called them "open and inadmissible blackmail." President Zedillo tried to reassure his country with a speech that mentioned the word "sovereignty" nineteen times. "The highest aim of my government is the full exercise of national sovereignty," he said. "We will accept no commitment that violates national sovereignty or threatens the legitimate interests of the Mexicans."[8]

Clearly, the high-handed approach that characterized U.S. dealings with Mexico in the nineteenth century is only likely to touch off a backlash of anti-American feeling today. Mexicans are proud of their country, which despite its troubles has emerged not only as a growing economic force but as an important political power, especially in Latin America. Mexico has played a key role in settling disputes between other Latin American countries, often taking stands that oppose U.S. policies in the region. For instance, it has maintained good relations with Cuba, despite the intense opposition of the United States to Cuba's Communist government.

However, the fact that the United States can't dictate to Mexico doesn't mean that it has no influence over its southern neighbor. The reality is that economically and politically, the United States is still a powerful factor in Mexican society.

In the course of negotiating the peso bailout, U.S. officials won promises of better cooperation in stemming illegal immigration and drug trafficking. Mexican leaders also expressed a commitment to move toward fuller democracy.

Americans have always taken the view that democracy is the best guarantee of stability. Repressive systems, in which opposition groups are shut out of power, create social and political inequalities. They foster corruption, which increases crime as well as inequality and discontent. In theory, then, the surest way for the United States to solve the problems it faces with Mexico today is to promote greater democracy, as well as economic health, south of the border. But it can do that only by being mindful of Mexican concerns. To benefit either country, the relationship between the United States and Mexico must be built on mutual respect.

MEXICO AND THE UNITED STATES: A CHRONOLOGY

1521 The Spanish conquistador Hernán Cortés captures Tenochtitlán, the Aztec capital, on the site of present-day Mexico City.

1598 Spanish settlers under Juan de Oñate found San Juan de los Caballeros on the banks of the Rio Grande.

1607 Jamestown, Virginia, England's first permanent colony in North America, is founded.

1610 The Spanish found the city of Santa Fe to serve as the capital of the province of New Mexico. Spain gradually extends its rule over all or part of the present-day states of Arizona, Colorado, New Mexico, Texas, Nevada, and Utah.

1680 Pueblo Indians rebel; they occupy Santa Fe until 1693, when they are driven out.

1769 Spanish priests and soldiers found the Mission of San Diego, the first of a string of Roman Catholic missions that help colonize California under Spanish rule.

1783 The United States wins independence from Great Britain.
1803 The United States doubles its size by acquiring the Louisiana Territory from France.
1821 Mexico wins independence from Spain. The Mexican government grants Stephen Austin of Missouri permission to bring settlers from the United States into Texas.
1835 United States-born Texas settlers rebel against Mexico and win independence, establishing the Lone Star Republic.
1845 Texas joins the United States as the twenty-eighth state.
1846 A border dispute sparks fighting between Mexico and the United States. The United States declares war in May; in June, American settlers in California declare independence from Mexico and establish the Bear Flag Republic.
1847 United States forces under General Winfield Scott take Mexico City.
1848 Under the Treaty of Guadalupe-Hidalgo, ending the Mexican War, Mexico cedes to the United States nearly half its territory, an expanse that includes all or part of ten present states.
1849 Thousands of people pour into California in search of gold.
1854 The Gadsden Purchase transfers an additional strip of territory from Mexico to the United States.
1855 Mexican president Antonio López de Santa Anna is driven from power for the last time.
1861 Benito Juárez, a liberal reformer, emerges victorious after years of civil strife in Mexico. In the United States, the Civil War begins.

1862 French troops invade Mexico; they take Mexico City the following year and establish a monarchy, with Archduke Maximilian of Austria on the throne.

1865 The U.S. Civil War ends. The United States begins to supply arms to Juárez, who is fighting the French. French troops pull out the next year.

1867 Maximilian is captured and shot; Juárez returns to power.

1876 Porfirio Díaz becomes president of Mexico, beginning a thirty-four-year-long rule during which United States investment will play an important role in the country.

1885 United States–Mexican cooperation ends an Apache uprising, led by Geronimo, in the border region.

1910 Francisco Madero, Pancho Villa, Emiliano Zapata, and others rebel against Díaz, who flees Mexico the next year.

1913 Victoriano Huerta overthrows Madero and becomes president. Civil war continues.

1914 The United States sides against Huerta. President Woodrow Wilson sends marines to block arms shipments at the port of Veracruz. Huerta flees the country three months later, but civil war continues.

1916 Pancho Villa's band attacks Americans and American settlements along the border. In response, U.S. troops pursue Villa deep into Mexico.

1917 The United States withdraws its troops from Mexico as it prepares to enter World War I. Mexico adopts the constitution of 1917, which calls for land reform and other liberal changes.

1924 The U.S. Border Patrol is formed to police immigration from Mexico.

1930 Mexico nationalizes foreign-owned oil wells.

1942 The Bracero Program begins, bringing Mexican contract workers to the United States. It lasts into the 1960s.

1954 United States officials round up one million Mexicans in a crackdown on illegal immigration.

1969 The United States launches Operation Intercept to halt drug traffic on the border.

1976 Oil begins to bring new wealth to Mexico; by 1981, it accounts for three-fourths of the country's total exports, with the United States the biggest buyer.

1982 Unable to make payments on its mounting foreign debt, Mexico is plunged into a financial crisis. The United States helps arrange new loans in exchange for economic reforms.

1986 The U.S. Immigration Reform and Control Act offers amnesty to some illegal aliens but provides stiff penalties to employers who hire undocumented workers.

1991 Mexican soldiers, apparently protecting an illegal drug shipment, shoot government drug agents in an incident that reflects the growing hold of drug traffickers on the country.

1993 Canada, Mexico, and the United States sign the North American Free Trade Agreement (NAFTA), which lowers trade barriers between them.

1994 • NAFTA takes effect.
• Rebellion breaks out in the southern Mexican state of Chiapas.
• The Institutional Revolutionary Party (PRI) retains power in a presidential election that sees its first candidate shot dead at a Tijuana rally. Ernesto Zedillo Ponce de León, the party's second candidate, takes office in December.

- California voters adopt Proposition 187, a ballot initiative that would deny social services to illegal immigrants.

1995 After mounting debt again plunges Mexico into a financial crisis, the United States helps arrange a $50 billion rescue package. President Zedillo announces plans to increase democracy, attack corruption, and control drug trafficking.

1996 Mexican authorities and Chiapas rebels reach agreement on Indian rights. Juan Garciá Ábrego is extradited to the United States to face drug-trafficking charges.

SOURCE NOTES

CHAPTER 1

1. Dan McGraw, "Big Business Comes to the Border," *U.S. News & World Report* (Oct. 10, 1994), 100.

2. "Down Mexico Way," *The Economist* (April 18, 1992), A24.

3. Allen R. Myerson, "This Is the House That Greed Built," *New York Times* (April 2, 1995).

CHAPTER 2

1. Richard Henry Dana Jr., *Two Years Before the Mast* (Danbury, Conn.: Grolier, 1980), 81–82.

2. Ibid., 83.

3. Ibid., 170.

4. Quoted in Carter Smith, ed., *The Conquest of the West* (Brookfield, Conn.: Millbrook, 1992), 40.

5. Ibid., 46.

6. Paul R. Ehrlich, Loy Bilderback, and Anne H. Ehrlich, *The Golden Door: International Migration, Mexico, and the United States* (New York: Ballantine Books, 1979), 108.

7. Quoted in *America: Great Crises in Our History Told by Its Makers* (Chicago: Veterans of Foreign Wars, 1925), vol. 7, *The Mexican War and Slavery, 1845–1861*, 98.

8. Ehrlich, *The Golden Door*, 110.

9. Polk's diary entry of February 21, 1848, quoted in *America*, vol. 7, 104.

CHAPTER 3

1. Alan Riding, *Distant Neighbors: A Portrait of the Mexicans* (New York: Knopf, 1985), 318.

2. Ehrlich, *The Golden Door*, 115.

3. Ibid., 118.

4. Ibid., 142.

5. Ibid., 120.

6. Report by John Reed, quoted in Judith Adler Hellman, *Mexico in Crisis* (New York: Holmes and Meier, 1978), 9.

7. Wilson's address to Congress of August 27, 1913, reprinted in *America*, vol. 10, *A New World Power, 1890–1914*, 300.

8. Secretary of State Robert Lansing's official communication to the Mexican government, dated June 20, 1916, reprinted in *America*, vol. 12, *America in the Great War—and After, 1916–1925*, 15-16.

9. The Zimmerman Telegram, reprinted in *America*, vol. 12, 23.

10. Zapata's letter of March 1919, quoted in Hellman, *Mexico in Crisis*, 25.

11. Editorial from the New York *American*, quoted in Ehrlich, *The Golden Door*, 147.

CHAPTER 4

1. Riding, *Distant Neighbors*, 330.

2. Ibid., 331–332.

3. Abraham F. Lowenthal, *Partners in Conflict: The United States and Latin America* (Baltimore: Johns Hopkins University Press, 1987), 76.

4. "Return of the Nativist," *The Economist* (June 27, 1992), 25.

5. Ibid.

6. Sam Howe Verhovek, "With Detentions Up, Border Is Still Porous," *New York Times* (February 13, 1996).

7. Lucas Guttentag, Director, Immigrants' Rights Project of the American Civil Liberties Union, in a letter to the *New York Times* (August 30, 1995).

CHAPTER 5

1. George W. Grayson, "Mexico Today: A New Administration . . . New Challenges," *The Americana Annual 1995* (Danbury, Conn.: Grolier, 1995), 71.

2. Riding, *Distant Neighbors*, 147.

3. Statistics on the 1982 financial crisis in Riding, *Distant Neighbors*, 150.

4. Grayson, "Mexico Today," 73.

5. John Greenwald, "Surprise! NAFTA's Already Here," *Time* (November 15, 1993), 40.

6. *Facts on File World News Digest* (November 25, 1993), 875.

7. *Facts on File World News Digest* (November 18, 1993), 858.

8. United States Department of Commerce estimate cited in Dan McGraw, "Big Business Comes to the Border," *U.S. News & World Report* (October 10, 1994), 100.

CHAPTER 6

1. Chris Wood, "Borderline," *Maclean's* (July 19, 1993), 24.

2. Ibid.

3. Tim Golden, "Mexican Connection Grows as Cocaine Supplier to U.S.," *New York Times* (July 30, 1995).

4. Tim Golden, "To Help Keep Mexico Stable, U.S. Soft-Pedaled Drug War," *New York Times* (July 31, 1995).

5. Ibid.

6. Golden, "Mexican Connection."

CHAPTER 7

1. Anthony DePalma, "Mexicans Ask How Far Social Fabric Can Stretch," *New York Times* (March 12, 1995).

2. Ibid.

3. Andrew A. Reding, "It Isn't the Peso. It's the Presidency," *New York Times Magazine* (April 9, 1995), 54.

4. Linda Robinson and Lucy Congfer, "Mexico's New Revolution," *U.S. News & World Report* (August 15, 1994), 40.

5. Anthony DePalma, "Mexicans Bring Fear to the Ballot Box," *New York Times* (June 12, 1994).

6. Tim Golden, "Mexican Parties Sign Accord on Shift to Full Democracy," *New York Times* (January 18, 1995).

7. David E. Sanger, "With Opposition Rising, Clinton Pleads for Mexican Rescue Package," *New York Times* (January 19, 1995).

8. Tim Golden, "Mexicans Deny They Would Order Border Crackdown in Return for U.S. Loan Guarantees," *New York Times* (January 27, 1995).

FURTHER READING

*Barry, Tom, Harry Browne, and Beth Sims. *The Great Divide: The Challenge of U.S.–Mexico Relations in the 1990s.* New York: Grove Press, 1994.
*Catalano, Julie. *The Mexican Americans.* New York: Chelsea House, 1988.
*Dana, Richard Henry, Jr. *Two Years Before the Mast.* Danbury, Conn.: Grolier, 1980.
*Davis, Marilyn P. *Mexican Voices/American Dreams: An Oral History of Mexican Immigration to the United States.* New York: Henry Holt, 1990.
*Dublin, Thomas, ed. *Immigrant Voices: New Lives in America, 1773–1986.* Urbana, Ill.: University of Illinois Press, 1993.
*Ehrlich, Paul R., Loy Bilderback, and Anne H. Ehrlich. *The Golden Door: International Migration, Mexico, and the United States.* New York: Ballatine Books, 1979.
*Eisenhower, John S. D. *Intervention!: The United States and*

the Mexican Revolution, 1913–1917. New York: W.W. Norton, 1993.

*Hellman, Judith Adler. *Mexico in Crisis*. New York: Holmes and Meier, 1978.

*Jacobs, William Jay. *War With Mexico*. Brookfield, Conn.: Millbrook Press, 1993.

*Langewiesche, W. "The Border." *Atlantic* (May 1992), 53.

*Lowenthal, Abraham. *Partners in Conflict: The United States and Latin America*. Baltimore, Md.: Johns Hopkins University Press, 1987.

*Mayberry, Jodine. *Mexicans*. New York: Franklin Watts, 1990.

*Niblo, Stephen R. *War, Diplomacy, and Development: The United States and Mexico, 1938–1954*. Wilmington, Del.: Scholarly Resources, 1995.

*Oles, James. *South of the Border: Mexico in the American Imagination, 1914–1947*. Washington: Smithsonian Institution Press, 1993.

*Payne, Douglas W. "Mexico and Its Discontents." *Harper's Magazine* (April 1995), 68.

*Paz, Octavio. *The Labyrinth of Solitude*. New York: Grove Press, 1985.

*Poppa, Terrence E. *Druglord: The Life and Death of a Mexican Kingpin*. New York: Pharos Books, 1990.

*Raat, W. Dirk. *Mexico and the United States: Ambivalent Vistas*. Athens, Ga.: University of Georgia Press, 1992.

*Ribaroff, Margaret Flesher. *Mexico and the United States Today: Issues Between Neighbors*. New York: Franklin Watts, 1985.

*Riding, Alan. *Distant Neighbors: A Portrait of the Mexicans*. New York: Knopf, 1985.

*Skidmore, Thomas E., and Peter H. Smith. *Modern Latin America*. New York: Oxford University Press, 1984.

Smith, Clint E. *The Disappearing Border: Mexico–United States Relations to the 1990s.* Stanford, Calif.: Stanford Alumni Association, 1992.

Weintraub, Sidney. *A Marriage of Convenience: Relations Between Mexico and the United States.* New York: Oxford University Press, 1990.

Weisman, Alan. *La Frontera: The United States Border With Mexico.* San Diego: Harcourt Brace Jovanovich, 1986.

* These books are particularly suitable for younger readers.

INDEX

Ábrego, Juan García, 93, 97
agribusiness, 76–77
Alamo, 26–27
Arizona, 14, 36, 69
Austin, Stephen, 27

Bonior, David, 83
border crossings, 13–15, 57–58
Bracero Program, 62–63

California, 14, 24–25, 26, 28, 31, 35, 36, 65
Canada, 83, 84, 92
Cárdenas, Cuauhtémoc, 102–103
Cárdenas, Lázaro, 55, 74
Carranza, Venustiano, 48, 49, 50, 53, 54

Chapultepec Castle, 32–33
Chavez, Cesar, 63
Chiapas, Mexico, 100–101
Cinco de Mayo, 41
Ciudad Juárez, Mexico, 14
Civic Alliance, 102–103, 104
Civil War, United States, 42
Clinton, Bill, 83, 105
colonization, 22–23
Colosio, Luis Donaldo, 104
Commission for Environmental Cooperation, 92
Cortina, Juan Nepomuceno, 40

Dana, Richard Henry, 24–25
democracy, 107
Democratic Revolutionary Party (PRD), 102–103, 104

Díaz, Porfirio, 39, 42–43, 44, 45–46, 47, 74
drug-trafficking, 89–90, 93–97. *See also patrones*

economic issues, 18, 69–71, 77, 99–100, 105–107
environmental issues, 89–90, 90–93

factories. *See maquiladoras*
Frémont, John C., 31

Gadsden Purchase, 36
Gadsden, James, 36
Gallardo, Felix, 94–95
General Agreement of Tariffs and Trade (GATT), 81–82
Germany, 52–53
Gore, Al, 84
Grant, Ulysses S., 32–33
Grupo Beta, 70
Guadalupe-Hidalgo, Treaty of, 34–35, 36
Guttentag, Lucas, 70–71

Hidalgo y Costilla, Miguel, 23
Houston, Sam, 26–27
Huerta, Victoriano, 48, 49–50
Hurtado, Miguel de la Madrid, 81

illegal immigration, 61, 62, 63–64, 65, 66, 67, 87

immigration, 58–71
Immigration and Naturalization Service (INS), 67
Import Substitution Industrialization (ISI), 75
industry, growth of, 74–78
Institutional Revolutionary Party (PRI), 83, 100, 102–104
International Boundary and Water Commission (IBWC), 91–92
International Bridge, 14
International Monetary Fund (IMF), 80, 81, 86
investments in Mexico, American, 44–46
Iturbide, Augustín de, 23

Jones, James R., 97
Juárez, Benito, 41, 42

Know-Nothing Party, 59

La Reforma, 41
Lansing, Robert, 52
Ledo, Porfirio Muñoz, 83

Madero, Francisco, 46, 47–48
manifest destiny, 29, 58–59
maquiladoras, 15–16, 76, 82, 90, 91
Matamoras, Mexico, 90–91

Maximilian of Austria, Archduke, 42
Mexico City, 18, 23, 24, 33, 34, 36, 77–78
Monroe Doctrine, 42
NAFTA (North American Free Trade Agreement), 15, 73–74, 82–84, 85, 92, 96–97, 101, 105
Napoleon III, 41, 42
National Action Party (PAN), 104
Native American border conflict, 43–44
nativism, 59–60
New Mexico, 21–22, 31, 35, 36, 51
1986 Immigration Reform and Control Act, 66

Obregón, Alvaro, 54
oil industry, 53–55, 78–81
Oñate, Juan de, 21
OPEC (Organization of Petroleum Exporting Countries), 78, 79
Orozco, Pascual, 46, 47–48

patrones, 93–94
Perot, H. Ross, 73, 83–84
Pershing, John J., 51, 52
peso crisis, 85–87, 104
Pierce, Franklin, 36
Plan of San Diego, 50, 51

political issues, 102–104
Polk, James K., 29, 30, 31, 33, 34–35, 42
population growth, 78
Porfiriato, 43, 45, 47

railroads, 35–36, 44, 59
Rio Grande, 14–16, 21, 29, 30, 35, 39–40, 43, 51, 62, 90, 91
Roosevelt, Franklin D., 55

Salcido, Manuel, 94
Salinas de Gortari, Carlos, 81, 82, 103
San Juan de los Caballeros, 21
San Ysidro, California, 68–69
Santa Anna, Antonio López de, 23, 26–27, 31, 32, 33, 36
Santa Ysabel Massacre, 51
Scott, Winfield, 32, 33
seasonal farmworkers, 66–67
slavery, 25, 26, 27–28, 34, 40
social services, 67–68
Spanish empire, 22–25

Taylor, Zachary, 30, 31
Texas, 14–15, 16, 25–28, 29, 35, 36, 40, 68, 69, 79, 91
Texas Cart War, 40
Tijuana, Mexico, 14
Trist, Nicholas, 33–34

U. S. Congress, 28, 30, 48–49, 68, 84, 86, 103

U. S. Border Patrol, 61, 68–69, 70
United States, Mexico's perception of, 17

Villa, Pancho, 46–47, 48, 50–51

Walker, William, 36–37
Wilson, Henry Lane, 48
Wilson, Woodrow, 48–49
World War I, 52–53
World War II, 62, 75, 76, 81

Zapata, Emiliano, 47–48, 53
Zapatista National Liberation Army, 100–101
Zedillo Ponce de León, Ernesto, 85, 97, 104, 106
Zimmerman, Alfred, 52–53

ABOUT THE AUTHOR

Elaine Pascoe has served as staff newspaper writer, a senior reference book editor, and editor in chief of a children's book publishing company. From her base in western Connecticut, she now devotes her time to writing books and magazine articles.

Among her previous books for young adults are *Neighbors at Odds: U.S. Policy in Latin America* (named one of the "Best Books of 1990" by *School Library Journal*), *South Africa: Troubled Land*, and *Racial Prejudice*, which earned a certificate of merit from the National Council for the Social Studies.

Mexico & The United States

Elaine Pascoe

Lex: 1230 RL: 10.0   Pts: 8